"You c_____ r..."

Her breath hitched. "Maybe I wanted to be found, Mr. Maxwell."

"Did you now," he murmured.

"I bit my lip when you pulled me around." His mouth was so close to hers their lips brushed, featherlight, as she spoke.

"I apologize."

"Don't." Her pulse thundered. "Kiss it and make it better."

Tipping her chin up, he closed the distance between them.

Their lips slid together like two puzzle pieces clicking into place, solid and secure. Tongues touched, tentative yet growing bolder. Hands roamed, slow but desperate. And in no time at all, she was lost to the moment.

Seconds turned into minutes as he caressed her face, her neck, the upper swells of her breasts. He treated her like a sensual feast. Short breaths skated over her skin. When he slipped a hand under her shirt and deft fingers found one nipple, she gasped his name and let her head fall back.

Hunger. All she could think was that he made her hunger for him. Deprived of such sensual sensation for so long, she cou_____ than follow his lead in the _____ needed to get her feet und_____ would.

Dear Reader,

Welcome back to the world of Beaux Hommes, the hottest and most exclusive all-male revue in Seattle. It's Friday night, the place is packed and the music's just cuing up. You're in for a real treat, because the men who dance here? They know just how to crank the patrons up when they take it all off.

Writing the second book in this trilogy was an exciting challenge. It takes our hero out of the strip club environment for part of the book and places him in his first post-university job—the one he's dreamed of for so long it's become as familiar as a well-worn pair of jeans. He's comfortable with the opportunities he's created for himself. There's no doubt in his mind he'll be successful if he sticks to his five-year plan. Nothing is going to derail him from giving back to the same community service that saved his life all those years ago.

Enter the heroine, who just happens to be the conductor on the hero's train to contentment. She's not about to settle for his cautious plan when she finally finds herself in the arms of the one man she's craved for so long. Nope. Content just won't cut it, and settling isn't in her vocabulary.

This is a story of heartache and hope, but it's also about the power to be more than the sum of your past—whether you chose it or until you worked up the bravery to claim those things that always seemed out of reach. Particularly love.

Fondly,

Kelli Ireland

Kelli Ireland

Wound Up

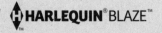
HARLEQUIN® BLAZE™

Recycling programs
for this product may
not exist in your area.

ISBN-13: 978-0-373-79832-2

Wound Up

Copyright © 2015 by Denise Tompkins

Printed in U.S.A.

From stable hand to a name on the door of a corporate American office, **Kelli Ireland** has been many things. (Never a waitress, however. Thank-you cards for her sparing the unsuspecting public from this catastrophe can be sent in care of her agent.) Writing has always been her passion, though. And writing romance? An absolute dream come true. Her theory is that a kiss should be meaningful regardless of length, a hero can say as much with a well-written look as he can with a long-winded paragraph and heroines are meant to hold their own. She's no Cinderella, and Shakespeare wrote the only *Romeo and Juliet*, so Kelli sticks to women who can save themselves and tortured heroes who are loath to let them.

Kelli and her husband live in the South, where all foods are considered fry-able and bugs die only to be reborn in bloodsucking triplicate. Visit her online at kelliireland.com anytime.

Books by Kelli Ireland

Harlequin Blaze

Pleasure Before Business

Stripped Down

Visit the Author Profile page at Harlequin.com for more titles

To Heather Tebbs, who has never met a challenge she couldn't conquer.

1

THE METRO TRANSIT belched a nauseating exhaust cloud as it pulled away from the curb. The transit authority might have a clean-fuel initiative, but Justin Maxwell couldn't breathe. He wiped his tearing eyes at the same time a luxury coupe sped by the bus stop and blanketed him in a sheet of gutter water.

Drenched and sputtering, he cursed. The first thing he was going to do when he started his new job next week was start saving to buy a car. It didn't have to be a sports car. It didn't even have to be a new car. Hell, he couldn't *afford* new. Just something with a roof, and doors and windows that didn't leak. Anything that kept him from having to take public transportation through the rotten Seattle weather.

No more crowding under bus stops to get out of the rain. No more shuffling through the bus's packed aisle to find space to stand. No more leaving his house an hour and a half early in order to make all his connections across town.

Hoisting his duffel over his shoulder, he trudged up Broad Street, cut across Third Avenue and slipped down the alley behind Beaux Hommes.

The front of the all-male revue was decidedly posh. From the back, though, the building looked like nothing more than unimpressive cinder block, barred windows and steel doors. Very industrial chic, if he ignored the rancid smells of the Dumpster and old restaurant grease from the Chinese place across the alley.

He jogged up the steps to the third door and entered his digital pass code. The keypad beeped, the lock clicked open and Justin slipped inside, heading for the locker room and the showers. No way could he hit the stage with the film of grime covering him.

Deep voices and masculine laughter echoed down the hall. As he shoved through the swinging door, he was met with shouts of welcome followed immediately by some serious ribbing about his grungy state.

"Hey, I can't help it if I'm better dressed on a bad day than the rest of you are on your best." He dumped his bag in his locker and began peeling off his wet clothes. Since he'd started at the club, he'd always been particular about the way he presented himself. It came from the lean years when clothes were too small because there hadn't been money to replace what he'd outgrown.

He was not that kid anymore.

Levi, a longtime friend and the club's lead dancer, sank onto the nearest bench and evaluated him dispassionately. "What the hell happened to you? You look like you've been rolling around in the alley. Brawling or balling?"

Justin snorted and scrubbed his hands over his hair, flinging water everywhere. "Neither."

"That's too bad." Levi stretched, lines of thick muscle quivering before he relaxed. "A little action before the show never hurts."

"Says the least discriminating man I know."

Levi stood, whipped his towel off and snapped it across the back of one of Justin's now-bare thighs.

He yelped and spun around. "You suck, Levi."

The dark-haired man grinned. "Only if they return the favor."

Justin shook his head and laughed. "I'm grabbing a quick shower. What's my rotation tonight?"

"You're fourth. You follow Nick. I follow you."

"Our resident shrink won't make any money shaking his junk after me," Nick called.

Justin laughed. "Right. Because your man boobs are bigger than mine." And they were. Nick was as tall as Justin at six-two, but he was a solid twenty pounds heavier and it was muscle stacked on muscle.

Nick stuck his head around the end of the lockers and made his pecs dance. "Don't hate on me because I'm built better."

Shrugging, Justin grabbed his shower caddy and slammed his locker. "Anyone can build a body, brother, but there's not a damn thing you can do about that face."

The room erupted in laughter, Nick included, and Justin headed for the open showers.

It surprised him to realize he would miss this, the camaraderie and feeling of brotherhood, when he cut back to working only a couple of nights a month. Graduating with his PhD meant he'd finally scored a more traditional, definitely more socially acceptable job. Beginning Monday, he would no longer be a full-time Beaux Hommes man but rather Dr. Justin Maxwell, staff psychologist for Second Chances, a nonprofit leadership initiative for disadvantaged inner-city youth. Receiving counseling from a licensed psychologist was a big part of the program.

He would know.

Hot water sluiced over his body as he soaped up, but the heat did little to ease his tension. All he wanted at the moment was to skip tonight's show, go home, get his stuff ready for Monday and then crash. But the efficiency apartment was brand-new to him. "New" really meant "empty." He'd bought a bed, but that was it. Save for that and a few pots and pans from a local thrift shop, the apartment was empty. He still funneled most of his earnings to his mom's house, covering the majority of the bills, making sure his sisters were fed and clothed. He owed them that much at least.

Resting his forearm against the tile wall, he let his chin fall forward so the shower stream pummeled his neck and shoulders.

Sixteen years. Sixteen years since the military had sent the chaplain to their door, and it still pissed him off. But thinking about it wasn't going to get him anywhere. He needed to get his game face on, dress and hit the weights before his first set.

Shutting the faucet off didn't stop the emotional trip down memory lane. He found himself considering who he was now versus who he'd been the first time he'd walked through the doors of Beaux Hommes on an open-call night ten years ago. He'd been working as a janitor for several weeks, watching the dancers' nightly cash take. When the next open call came for tryouts, he was there. He'd figured he'd get up on stage and show everyone how it was done and had brought a couple of his homeboys with him to yuck it up when he was finished. Mistake number one. The lead dancer hadn't even looked at Justin twice. He'd not even set foot on the stage before the guy called out, "Pass."

Furious, Justin had got up in the guy's grill. Mistake number two.

The lead dancer hadn't backed down, didn't even bat a damn eye. He'd come at Justin, drilling his finger into his chest. "Grow a pair, and I don't mean Leftie and Rightie over there, and you can audition again. If, and I do mean *if*, you cut clean now."

Justin's anger, always simmering so close to the surface then, had boiled over. "You're calling my boys—"

"Your testicles. Yes, I'm calling them your testicles. If

you've got to wear 'em on your sleeve, this isn't the job for you. Get out."

Ego bruised, he'd gone home, stewed over it for a few days and then talked to his counselor about the opportunity. With support from Second Chances, he'd come back. Alone. They'd hired him with one major caveat: the stuff they suspected he was dabbling in—gangs, guns and girls—could never, *ever* come to work with him. He'd had a choice in that moment. Clean up and make a decent living at twenty, or turn to the streets full-time. Most of the Deuce-8 crew didn't live to see thirty. It wasn't much of a choice.

Bracing a fist against the shower wall, Justin grinned and shook his head. He'd been an idiot that first night, thinking he was all that while living fast and hard amid gunfire and turf wars. "Idiot" didn't even begin to cover it.

Grabbing his towel, he dried off as muffled, bass-heavy music drifted through the locker room. The first screams from the crowd went up. His stomach did the ever-familiar flip. Dancing for dollars would never be second nature to him the way it was to Levi, but the money had always been as good as they'd promised. And he had a large debt to repay—to his mom and to Second Chances.

He grabbed his first costume. Time to pay a few bills.

JUSTIN STOOD IN the wings and waited. Nick's routine was almost over, and the stagehands had swept up cash twice already. It would be a nice take.

Levi slipped in beside Justin, wearing his fireman costume—a crowd favorite. "We've got a full house tonight."

That stomach flip thing happened again. Justin hated the tension of standing around waiting. It was easier to show up as the other guy's set was ending. Then he could simply walk onstage as soon as his props were set. But Levi had rearranged a few things when he'd recently bought into the club as a partner, and one of those things was that the next dancer had to be ready and waiting off stage in order to prevent delays. Despite Justin's irritation, he had to admit it worked well. They'd been able to add in two extra routines a night, and that meant higher revenues for everyone involved. Still, it didn't do anything for his butterflies other than give them sharp-edged wings.

The dark-haired man glanced over. "Seems odd this is your last regular weekend."

"Yeah." Justin ran a hand around his neck and pulled hard enough his arm shook with the strain. "It won't change too much, though."

"We'll see."

Assessing the crowd, Justin's gaze skipped from face to face as he considered his routine. He recognized a few regulars who tipped well. He'd work their seats hard. A couple of tables sported bride sashes and tiaras—wedding groups were always good money. Those were added to his front list. The rest of the tables were crowded with unfamiliar faces. He'd watch those customers, see how they responded to him and react accordingly.

Guilt burned in his belly. This was the part he hated, casing the crowd like some damn dollar-bill desperado, deciding who was worth the bulk of his time after just a couple of quick passes.

He'd learned the skill on the streets, how to single out the best chump or the weakest link. Using that skill now left him feeling tainted, as if he was selling not only his body but his hard-won integrity, as well. Such a long way he'd come, climbing out of the gutter only ten years ago. It was a lifetime and just yesterday.

"Does it ever bother you?" he asked quietly. "What we do?"

Levi didn't look at him when he answered but kept his eyes on the crowd. "No. We're feeding a fantasy for them, a craving to desire and be desired. As a psychologist, you know that better than any of us." When Justin didn't immediately answer, the taller man glanced his way. "What's bugging you?"

"Not sure."

"You need to get laid."

Justin grinned and shook his head. "That's your answer for everything."

"I'm serious. When was the last time you got some?"

"Been a while."

"You don't even remember, do you?"

Justin shrugged uncomfortably. "I just got a bed. What was I supposed to do before that, Levi? Ask a woman if she wanted to go back to my empty place and fool around on the floor? That was bound to garner a hell of a lot of yeses."

Levi turned to him. "You have to blow off some steam, enjoy life a little more than you have over the past, oh, *decade plus*. You've done nothing but take care of your family and go to school. You worked your ass off and you've made it, man. Monday begins a new chapter in your life. Take tonight and just enjoy yourself. Once every ten years or so won't kill you."

"Funny." But Justin knew Levi was at least partially right. He'd done nothing but work: as a student and teacher's assistant on campus during the day and as a stripper Thursday through Saturday nights. There hadn't been time for indulgences.

Looking over the crowd, his gaze landed on a stunning auburn-haired woman. Bright, cat-shaped eyes tilted up at the corners. She wore very little makeup. Full lips, high cheekbones, pert nose, an elegant neck—everything he could see made his blood hum through his veins. She smiled at the woman beside her, revealing a flash of white teeth and a single dimple.

"Well, what do you know," he murmured. It was Grace

Cooper, the only student who had ever come close to convincing him to break the ethics clause in his teaching assistant's contract with the university. And she hadn't even been aware she was doing it. She'd just shown up to class and been beautiful, lusciously curvy and decidedly brilliant.

They'd flirted—a brush of a hand here, a gentle touch there, an undisguised look caught before it was cloaked. He'd come so close to asking her out. She had been everything he'd wanted in a woman. Still was. And the want was still there, burning just beneath the surface.

But he was no longer her instructor, no longer bound by honor to keep his desires to himself. He could pursue her. Here. Tonight. Now.

His previous plan went out the window as he mentally amended his routine. "I'm switching gears," he said to Levi. "Tell the DJ to cue up the song for my new set. And I'm going to need a chair."

The other man shifted to see what Justin was staring at. He whistled. "Hottie at one o'clock."

Justin stepped into Levi's line of sight. "One warning— hands off."

Levi grinned and held his hands out, palms open. "Got it."

"Great. Now get me a chair and make sure the DJ switches up the song."

Justin's conscience reared, ready to argue, but lust sucker-punched the bastard before it could draw a solid breath. He'd played by the rules for the past three years where she was concerned. And this was his last night before he joined the eight-to-five world. Once, just once, he wanted to live a little.

For the first time in his life, taking it off felt as natural as breathing.

GRACE COOPER SANK back in her chair and pushed her mass of hair over one shoulder. This had been the best possible way to spend the weekend. Hands down. Stealing some down time and allowing herself to splurge for once had been critical to her mental health. As an almost psychologist, she would know.

She'd spent the day wandering the waterfront with her friends. Pike Place had the most amazing flower market, and she'd caved, buying a bouquet of daisies for the kitchen. Then there had been the crepe restaurant for dinner. Holy. Crow. So good. She was still full. And now this, the pinnacle of the weekend. Gorgeous men taking their clothes off, a little benign flirting and some innocent fun with her girlfriends before they left the city and started careers in different parts of the country.

Meg, her best friend, leaned over and tapped her shoulder. "Best. Idea. Ever."

Grace laughed. "You need a bib. You've got a little something right—" she dragged her thumb across Meg's chin "—there."

Meg grimaced as heat burned across her cheeks. "Did you *see* Nick?"

"Just as much of him as you did."

"I've never seen a man move that way." Meg fanned herself. "I'd come back frequently if I wasn't moving to Baltimore."

"And I'll be following you as soon as this practicum is over." Grabbing her margarita, she took a healthy sip.

Two weeks. After that, she had some decisions to make. The kinds of decisions she'd been looking forward to making for as long as she could remember. She was moving to Baltimore with Meg, completely stepping away from the life she'd been trapped in since birth and becoming something, some*one*, more. All she'd ever wanted was the ability to choose for herself who she'd be instead of living as an unwanted by-product of her mother's environment and choices.

Determination was all she'd had to see her through the hard years, the hungry nights, the lonely holidays. And if determination had carried her this far, there was no reason to think it wouldn't carry her as far as she wanted to go. She'd carve out her own niche, do something special after a life that had been less than noteworthy. If only she could figure out what, and where, her niche *was*. There wasn't room to make a mistake—not with the deferment of her student-loan payments ending and her housing situation dire for the next two weeks.

Frowning into her glass, she fought the urge to curse. She'd been forced to move in with her mother when the man she and Meg had been subletting their apartment from returned from his Doctors Without Borders trip early. It wasn't a big deal for Meg; she'd just gone home. It was more…complicated for Grace. Home had never been the safe place it was supposed to be. The word had never conjured feelings of security, and it had never been a place of refuge. Her mother had only been a parent in the biological sense. Nurture and love had never been part of that woman's vocabulary.

She rolled her head back and forth and took a deep breath. *Two weeks. You can do anything for two weeks.*

"Ladies, you're in for a real treat." The MC's voice, deep and dark, dragged her out of her reverie and settled the crowd's chatter to an anxious hum. "It seems a Beaux Hommes crowd favorite has decided to unveil a new alter ego this evening, and he's going to be choosing one lucky lady to help with the introductions."

"I wonder if Nick would understand if I volunteered," Meg murmured.

Grace chuckled, watching as the spotlight whisked across the crowd. Hands were up in the air, women waving like crazed matadors in the face of angry bulls as they tried to garner the operator's attention. She shook her head and bent forward to grab her purse. Virgin or not, her drink could use refreshing. Might as well do it while they were setting up for the next dancer.

Air whispered around her as the owner of black wing-tips stopped in front of her chair. She froze. Cologne, musky and rich, tickled her nose. The spotlight pinpointed her, and she swore it burned hot as the noonday sun.

A work-roughened finger hooked under her chin and gently lifted.

This was *not* happening. She didn't *want* to be chosen to help the policeman or chef or magician or whatever he was going to be dressed as take off his clothes. She just wanted to watch. And tip. And watch some more. But be part of the act? No.

In spite of herself, she let her head tilt back and slowly took him in. Her eyes raked across a tall, hard body. He pulled her up until she stood in front of him. Subtle pressure encouraged her to meet his gaze. Shock made her draw in a sharp breath.

Dark brows arched elegantly over pale blue irises ringed in navy blue. His lashes were so thick she almost hated him. Almost. His jaw was chiseled. The way his mouth tipped up at one corner said he smiled regularly, and she had the strangest urge to see that smile now. Not his stage smile, but a genuine one. His lower lip was full, made for nibbling, while his upper lip formed a perfect cupid's bow. She couldn't stop staring at his mouth—no surprise. It had always been this way with him.

"Justin Maxwell," she whispered. The one man in the world she'd hungered for on every level. The one man who had been out of reach for three years. Every cell in her body heated until a fine sheen of sweat decorated the nape of her neck. She licked her lips as her breath came short. How could *he* be *here*? Tonight? Why? And why couldn't he be wearing more clothes when he touched her?

He tipped his fedora in acknowledgment, leaving it sitting at a cocky angle. "I'll need you to come with me, Ms. Cooper."

The soft timbre of his voice whispered through her, caressing and igniting parts of her that had no business being on fire.

Grace opened her mouth to politely decline. Yes, she'd harbored a major crush on the man for years, but that didn't mean she'd hop on stage with him at his request. No, she couldn't. "Absolutely, Professor."

"Never was a professor, and I'm not standing in front of anyone's whiteboard anymore, sweetheart." And she wasn't sitting in a lecture hall anymore, either.

Her stomach flipped over as anxiety landed dead center in her belly.

Taking her hand, he backed through the crowd with confident steps, as if he knew exactly who and what was behind him.

He led her up a short set of stairs and stood her in the middle of the stage. "Don't think about the crowd. Focus on me. I'll take care of you," he said quietly.

Her inner wild child stretched and purred, tired of being put in a box over the years as she'd busted her ass to earn her undergraduate and graduate degrees. Now all that wild part of her wanted was a piece of him. "I'll hold you to that."

That coveted smile pulled at one corner of his mouth. "Please do."

She gave a short nod, and he raised a hand as he stepped away from her. The lights immediately dimmed and several women screamed while others whistled.

Music started, soft at first. Initially it had a digital feel, and then the first electric guitar cords drowned out the synthesizer. Bass guitar dropped in with a deep, almost drumming line. The music hammered at her nerves, lighting her up from the inside and making her hyperaware of the way her clothes rubbed over her skin.

The spotlight flashed on, narrow at first and then widening to show Justin moving toward her in a Milan-worthy stalk-walk through the artificial smoke billowing across the stage. His feet hit the floor in time with the music. He flicked his trench coat open, letting it billow behind him as he moved. Tuxedo-style pants were held up with black suspenders. He wore a cummerbund of white satin. And that was it. His bare chest showcased his warm skin and ripped physique. He wasn't huge but, damn, she would have given just about anything to trail her fingers over his defined pecs and down those rippling abs.

She glanced at his face and froze.

His eyes were hot, his smile one of pure seduction. He arched a brow as he closed in on her.

Grace licked her lips again, the action partly nerves but predominately anticipation. She wanted his hands on her in the worst way and, surprisingly, it turned her on to know that other people were watching.

As if he'd heard her thoughts, his eyes grew hooded. He stalked her in an ever-tightening circle. Whipping his coat off, he flung it to the side as the lyrics settled around her in a haze of lust. The singer was instructing the woman in the song to beg. But instead of encouraging Grace to go to her knees, Justin did.

He dropped behind her and ran broad hands up the backs of her legs, over her ass and settled them at her waist, making her skin suddenly feel too tight. His hot breath skated along the hollow of her spine as his thumbs lifted the hem of her shirt and he placed his firm lips against the soft sway of her back.

She involuntarily arched.

Strong hands tightened around her waist, holding her still. The tip of his tongue traced the tiniest line up her skin.

A whimper caught in her throat. Heat flooded her sex.

He moved behind her, scaling her body like a half-naked superhero.

She absently wondered what his superpower would be and realized, without a doubt, it would be the power of seduction. The power to make her crave him. The power to make her beg if he wanted her to.

Smooth hands slid under her shirt and up her belly. Thumbs traced ghost-like over the lower swells of her breasts. Her nipples pearled.

Lost to the sensations, her eyes fluttered shut.

Then he was gone.

Her head snapped around, searching for him.

He'd moved into the shadows near the edge of the stage to retrieve a chair. Pushing it toward her, he moved with lithe grace. His skin gleamed, pulled taut over those defined muscles, and his eyes burned as his lips curled with that superpower, seduction. And the closer he came, the hotter she got.

Three things hit Grace all at once.

One, she genuinely wanted this man in every sense of the word *want*.

Two, she was going to have him.

Three, she was going to enjoy every minute and consider the consequences later.

2

JUSTIN HADN'T TAKEN his rip-away tuxedo pants off yet. He should have. The routine called for it. But he couldn't. Not until he got his cock under control. The minute he laid his lips to the small of Grace's back, that traitor had stopped listening to his demand to stand down. Primal hunger had roared through him at the slight taste of salt on her skin. Then the faint musk of her arousal had punched his lust up to uncontrollable levels. Never had he responded to a woman this way. Something about her made him lose control, and, as usual, that both fascinated and irritated him. He was famed for his control.

Seating her in the chair, he went to his knees in front of her, legs spread wide. He leaned back on one hand and pumped his hips toward her. Sure, his arousal was apparent—she might as well know up front. Keeping things the way they'd always been was no longer an option. Now that she'd seen him here, had discovered that he danced, the knowledge couldn't be taken back. He was going to run with it as far and fast as he could go before she called stop. For the first time since he'd started dancing, he wanted the patron, *this* patron, to see him as available.

Her eyes locked on his groin. Then they dragged their way up his body to meet his.

The sheer hunger that smoldered in their depths stole his breath.

"Touch me." The words were out of his mouth without a thought.

"Beg."

His balls tightened at the command. So she was listening to the song, was she?

He grinned, putting every ounce of predatory sensuality into it he could muster as he rose to his knees and got in her face. "You'll regret that."

"Make me."

"Done." Raw, sexual hunger surfed the arousal flooding his veins. Wave after wave of desire pulsed through him. Crawling around her, he prowled up her body slowly, bent to her ear and breathed, "Please."

A hard shiver worked through her.

Justin pulled her into his arms and switched places with her, settling her across his lap. Hips thrusting, he pantomimed raw sex as his hands ran down her hips. The heat of her sex bled through his thin pants and he wanted nothing more than to touch her there, to find out if she was as wet as he wanted her to be. His hands shook. "Please," he said, louder this time.

Smooth hands ran over his chest.

He lifted his chin and watched her. The way her eyes locked on his torso, the way her fingertips traced every contour of his body—it fueled his need for her. Wrapping his arms around her ass, he surged to his feet.

Her eyes widened, locking on his.

Moving his face toward hers was natural. He leaned in until their lips almost touched. "Please." The whispered plea made their lips touch for a split second, but it was enough. She tasted like fresh lime, tart and sweet. Such a heady mix.

She gasped as he spun and set her in the chair again. Moving away, he toed his shoes off one at a time, kicking them clear and, with his back to the crowd, ripped his pants off.

She sank her teeth into her bottom lip even as her nostrils flared. The message was clear. She wanted him.

So he danced for her.

Facing Grace, he went to his knees and ran his hands over his body. He rolled a finger out and curled it in a "come here" motion.

She stood and walked toward him with exaggerated steps, her movements in perfect sync with the music. The way she moved, all sultry confidence, made his blood boil. When she reached him, he settled on his heels and pulled her forward to straddle him. He thrust upward, sliding his free hand up her front. Then he slid through her legs, jumped up and moved in behind her. Gripping her hips, he bent her forward some and folded his body over hers, settling his erection in the crevice of her ass.

She shivered.

Or it might have been him.

The music ended and the lights went out.

He grabbed her hand and headed for the wings. She kept up, never balking, and he was relieved. Hunger burned low in his gut. He wanted her so badly he was terrified he might actually throw her over his shoulder and run away with her. To where, he had no idea. Probably the first hotel he came across.

The Spartan decor of the back of the stage was at total odds with the plush interior out front. They nearly ran down a long corridor, his hand clinging to hers. Several performers called out greetings as they passed.

He ignored them.

Without warning, he slid to a stop and pulled her into a corner.

Grace crashed into him.

Justin spun, grabbed her and pressed her up against the wall. "I need you."

Wide, green eyes stared up at him, her pupils blown with desire. "Feeling's mutual."

Twining their fingers together, he dragged her hands over her head. She arched into him, and he groaned. His lips met hers in a desperate duel for dominance. Her mouth offered endless pleasure while her body smelled like sin. She rubbed against him, hooking one leg around his as he wedged a thigh between hers. Her soft mewl was nearly his undoing.

He craved her so badly and felt slightly guilty for dragging her back here without even talking to her first. If someone had treated either of his little sisters this way? Hell, he'd kill them. The shock of his behavior washed over him as effectively as a bucket of ice water. This was no way to treat a woman he liked and respected, a woman he'd wanted to ask out for three years. Jerking back, he stared down at her, panting. "I'm sorry."

"No talking." She leaned up and reclaimed his mouth, nipping his bottom lip before soothing the sting with the tip of her tongue. "Not yet."

He pulled away. "I don't do this. Ever."

She sighed, and relaxed against the wall. "Believe it or not, neither do I."

Dropping his forehead to hers, he closed his eyes. "Want to get out of here?"

"Yeah."

"I'll meet you out front in ten minutes."

She kissed him quickly. "Make it eight." Then she pulled her hands free and slipped under his arm, heading back the way they'd come, hips swaying hypnotically.

"Door to the club's on the right," he called.

She raised a hand in acknowledgment but never slowed down.

With a huff, he pushed off the wall and jogged toward the locker room.

He figured he had six minutes to come up with a decent plan that ended with her naked in his arms.

He'd borrow Levi's car, though it rankled that he didn't have his own. They could go to a late dinner. Maybe add something fun in there. Or a trip to his favorite dessert place for something sweet. The little restaurant he had in mind wasn't fancy but it was intimate. They could talk. He could show her he was better than the sum of his behavior so far tonight.

A dark smile spread across his face as he headed for his locker.

Maybe he'd go straight for the kill shot and try to talk her into breakfast…tomorrow morning.

GRACE SLIPPED TO her table where her girlfriends were chattering like songbirds.

Meg reached out and grabbed her by the wrist. "Holy crap, girl! You're the luckiest woman I know."

"Yeah?" She grabbed her purse. "I'm about to get luckier."

"Shut up." Lynn, a close friend, leaned across the table. "You aren't going out with him."

"Nope." She grinned and let the wickedness of her thoughts show. "I have the distinct impression we'll be spending the evening in."

Meg whooped and Lynn laughed. Gretchen, the most levelheaded of the group, sipped her drink and watched Grace over the rim of her glass. "You think this is a good idea? You don't know him."

"I actually sort of do." They clamored for more information, but she waved them off. "We met in the psychology department. No, I had no idea he danced here. Yes, he's a fantastic kisser. No, you won't get more details than that, so don't ask." She looked at Gretchen. "Just this once, I want to live a little."

Gretchen nodded. "I get that. I do." She took another sip, her brow furrowing as Grace watched. "And I can't believe I'm saying this, but you could do worse than living it up with a stripper."

The muscles in Grace's neck tightened and made her nod sharp. "Right."

All three women were silent at her words. That they felt sorry for her chafed. Her chin went up. "I'll check in with you guys tomorrow."

Gretchen lifted her glass, the casual gesture at direct odds with the concern reflected in her eyes. "Promise you'll be careful. Oh, and take my smartphone. Your by-the-minute phone is great if you have time to call for help, but in the event he's an ax murderer? It's useless. I'll turn on the 'find me' feature so I can recover your body if necessary."

Grace accepted the phone as she stood. "I have no idea where we'll go, but I'm guessing his place. If the phone takes off at a high rate of speed in the next couple of hours? Come after me." She glanced at her watch. "Gotta go."

She tried to keep her pace casual and controlled as she headed for the front door. In truth, though, she wanted to run. Despite her best efforts, her strides lengthened until she was charging through the club. Several women commented on her passing. Most of the words were benign if a little jealous, but some were downright mean. Grace didn't slow down. She wasn't going to allow herself to apologize for wanting sex, for enjoying it and for taking advantage of the moment. Had she been a man, she'd have been admired for the conquest. As a woman, she wasn't about to apologize for the same. Justin would be *her* conquest as much as she'd be his.

Cool air heavy with mist washed over her as she pushed

through the club's front doors. She stopped and slowly turned.

Staring at the ground in front of him, Justin came around the corner of the building wearing a knee-length trench over jeans and a white T-shirt. His chin came up, and his eyes narrowed.

She started for him without thinking.

They came together on the sidewalk, her arms going around his neck at the same time he lowered his mouth to hers. The kiss was swift but sure.

"Hi," he said softly.

"Hi, yourself."

He searched her face.

Her brows drew together. "Problem?"

"No. Just…" He shrugged.

Unease curled through her belly. She stepped a pace away.

Justin caught her hand. "I feel bad for nearly accosting you." He raked his fingers through his hair and stared over her shoulder, refusing to meet her gaze. "I want you to know I'm a better man than that."

"Hey." She tipped her head to the side and grabbed his attention. "I'm perfectly capable of saying no."

"Yeah, but—"

Laying her fingers across his lips, she shook her head. "No."

"What I meant was—"

"No." She pulled her hand away. "See? I told you I'm good at saying it."

He arched a brow and his lips twitched.

"I mean it, Justin. Short of a brief but intimate introduction to my tonsils and your insider knowledge of my grades in Psych 410, 510 and 525, we're strangers. You'll have to trust I know myself well enough to ask for what I need." Closing the distance between them, she placed one hand over his heart and ran the other around his neck. With soft pressure, she pulled him close. "And what I want is you." She laid her lips over his in a tender kiss.

He responded with unerring skill, moving over her lips to her jaw and laying small kisses all the way to her ear. "Might I interest you in grabbing some dinner?"

Her heart lodged in her throat at the question. The most she could manage was a small shake of her head. The hitch in his breath made her curl her fingers into the short wisps of hair at the nape of his neck. "I've already eaten."

"I'm starving."

Desire wove through those two simple words, and she understood it wasn't just food he craved. She leaned into him. He wrapped his arms around her, and she reveled in his strength as he pulled her even closer. The scent of laundry detergent from his clothes mingled with his cologne to give him a clean, masculine smell she loved.

He rested his chin atop her head and stroked her back in an achingly tender gesture. "I'd like to grab something to eat. I want to do this right. We can decide where to go from there, okay?"

"What sounds good to you?"

"I need protein and carbs. Dancing burns me out." He pulled away and, cupping her jaw, tipped her face up to his. "You did really well on stage."

"Thanks. So did you."

His head fell back as he laughed. Settling, he grinned down at her. "You didn't tip me."

"Maybe I'm holding out for a private performance."

Blue eyes darkened with desire. "I bet we can arrange something after I eat."

Grace traced the planes of his chest through the soft cotton of his shirt, thinking. She could play this any number of ways. Games weren't her style, though. Direct communication was much more in line with her preferences. So…

taking a deep breath, she met his gaze head on. "I suppose there's dinner or…breakfast."

Justin's heart tripped beneath her palm before it began to hammer against his rib cage. His lips parted, but he said nothing.

"Or we could—"

"Breakfast is perfect." Lacing their fingers together, he lifted their joined hands to his lips and gently kissed her knuckles. "Did you drive tonight?"

"I actually rode with friends." She pulled free and began to dig in her purse, determined to find Meg's cell phone. "I can call a cab."

Justin was quiet before saying, "I've got a car in paid parking."

Something in his voice made her look up. "Are you sure?"

His smile was a little too bright. "I'm pretty sure that's where it is."

She searched his face but that smile never wavered. "Okay."

He draped an arm over her shoulders and started across the street. Halfway there, his steps faltered briefly. Dropping his arm, he started walking toward the parking garage again. "Sixth floor unfortunately. It was crowded tonight."

The urge to poke at him a little, to figure out why the mention of the car had irritated him, almost overwhelmed her. Instead, she followed him to the elevator.

The minute the doors started to slide shut, he rounded on her. "For the record? Just because I'm slowing this down a little doesn't mean I'm not desperate for you. We clear?"

She dropped her purse and took an involuntary step back as he closed in, wove his hands through her hair and descended on her mouth with obvious intent. All she could do was grip his jacket and hold on.

Justin owned her mouth, his tongue delving inside hers

with breath-stealing eroticism. He tasted of spearmint mouthwash. He felt like the embodiment of temptation. He feasted on her, a man starving for her and only her. It was too much and not enough.

She gasped and arched into his hand when he cupped her breast and stroked a thumb over one aching nipple. Then he grabbed her ass and pulled her into his erection. His arousal was contagious. She was tinder to his flame and her body went up in a flash of female heat. A desperate moan escaped her tenuous control.

He swallowed the sound.

Their harsh breathing and sharp gasps filled her ears.

The elevator slid to a stop.

Justin lifted his head to wordlessly stare down at her.

The doors started to close.

He glanced over and hit the button to hold them open.

"I thought you were hungry," she said softly.

"I might have been wrong."

His stomach chose that moment to growl. He cursed.

"Forget breakfast. The sooner we get you fed, the sooner we can…" Heat burned across her cheeks. *Damn fair complexion.*

The skin of his thumb was slightly rough as he caressed her cheek. "We're both adults, Grace. Unless you're talking about a Monopoly marathon, I would imagine we're on the same page."

"Yay, adulthood," she whispered.

He grinned. Whatever bothered him earlier had disappeared. "Yay, adulthood, indeed." Swooping low, he grabbed her purse in one hand and settled the other on her waist. "Let's go, beautiful."

Grace stepped out of the elevator and followed him across the concrete pad. She could give herself this one night. On Monday she'd start her two-week practicum, the last thing she was required to complete in order to earn her diploma. Then she'd start her life in Baltimore. She'd be free. So, yeah, she would enjoy tonight. Maybe she could talk Justin into grabbing something at a drive-through so they could get to Monopoly faster. She wondered if he'd chosen the long-running game for a reason.

She could only hope.

3

NAVIGATING FIRST THE parking garage's hairpin turns and then Seattle's waterfront traffic, Justin's mind wandered over the woman in the borrowed Camaro's passenger seat. The fact that she had let him take the lead had been appealing at first. It only became an issue when she didn't offer to drive or take him to her place. What was he going to do? He couldn't take her to his apartment. A hotel he could afford would seem sleazy. A hotel he *couldn't* afford was irresponsible. He could ask her if she was interested in taking this to her place, but that seemed overtly presumptuous, even in the face of their conversation. There was always the chance Levi would let Justin use his pad, but that felt worse than a cheap hotel. He supposed he might—

"What sounds appealing?"

He couldn't stop the tightening of his hands on the steering wheel any more than he could change his immediate response. "You."

Her sultry laugh nearly undid him. "I was thinking more along the lines of food, like drive-through versus restaurant."

Heart pounding out a tribal rhythm in his brain, he chanced a glance at her. He nearly blew a vein. Her eyes were radiant in the streetlights, her skin nearly translucent. She nibbled her lower lip. Her palms were rubbing up and down her thighs, and he doubted she even realized it.

"I'm going to wreck this car if you don't stop looking at me like that," he murmured, returning his attention to the road.

"Like what?"

He grinned and shook his head. "Same way you used to look at me in class, making me forget what I was lecturing on." Reaching across the console, he fished for her hand, found it and brought it to his lips. Her skin was soft and smelled of shea butter and vanilla. "You used to make me wonder how you'd taste if I said 'to hell with it all' and kissed you in class."

Her hand tightened slightly around his. "Why didn't you?"

"Mostly? I needed the job. But there was also the other part of me, the curious part that wondered what might happen if we ever crossed paths outside of the university, where we had a chance to let things play out without being worried about the rules."

"I suppose now's the time to satisfy your curiosity. And mine."

He glanced at her, and all the blood in his brain dove south. "You've eaten dinner, but did you have dessert?"

"No."

"There's this great little dessert place in the market district. It might be crowded, but it's worth the wait if you're game."

"Sounds wonderful." She shifted toward him, resting on her hip. "How long have you danced at Beaux Hommes?"

He shrugged. "I started when I was twenty, so ten years."

"Wow."

"Why?" He chanced a quick glance at her as he wove through traffic.

"I just wondered how long I have to do penance for not realizing you danced there—and for not coming into the club and watching you sooner. Looks like I've got a decade to beat myself about the head and shoulders."

A short bark of laughter escaped him. "Enjoyed it that much, did you?" Spindly fingers of unease skittered along his spine. He would have preferred to keep his dancing and the club out of whatever happened between them.

Shoving her hair off her forehead, she nodded. "I enjoyed it way more than is probably legal in most states."

"Careful, Ms. Cooper. We can't afford to have the club shut down." He pulled into the café's parking lot and lucked into a space at the very front as another car left. "Out of curiosity, what would the charge have been?"

She didn't hesitate. "Unadulterated lust compounded by indecent thoughts in a public place."

The grin that stole over Justin was absolute. "You're quick."

This time she was the one who shrugged. "I've been suffering long enough to know."

Hand on the door handle, he paused. "Suffering?"

"Three years, Justin." Soft words in the car's semilit interior. "For three years I've watched you and laughed with you and wanted you. Remember when you had us get up, one at a time, to defend our theses? I bombed it because I couldn't stop staring at you. You were kind, and didn't call me out for my horrible delivery. I liked you even more for that, and I couldn't stop wondering if you were half as compelled as I was to skip class and play doctor." She smiled, the look somehow bittersweet. "I won't pretend it wasn't that way. Not now. Not anymore."

His heart lurched. "No. No more pretending." Drawing a deep breath, he pushed the door open. "Food first. Talk second." He glanced back. "And we'll discuss the specific terms of Monopoly."

"Deal." She slipped out of the car and met him at the door.

Taking her hand was entirely natural. He silently led her inside and snagged the first available table. A waitress was there in a heartbeat, and she immediately started to flirt with Justin, irritating him. The last thing he wanted was Grace to think he was an unconscionable jerk who had no respect for his date.

Date.

And that's really what this was. It had started as something different and evolved into him sitting across a table from her, watching her, wanting her. That last hadn't changed.

"Sir?" The waitress twirled her pen. "Does anything here sound…appetizing?"

Reaching across the table, he took Grace's hand and met her eyes when he answered. "Yeah, something here is just about perfect, but she's not on your menu."

Grace blushed, charming him to the core.

He lifted her hand to his mouth and kissed her knuckles. "I'll have a turkey club, no mayo, and fries. Grace?"

"I didn't read the menu."

"Do you like vanilla?"

"Yes."

"Do you trust me?"

She watched him, searching his eyes before answering. "Yes."

"My date and I will have the crème brûlée with fresh fruit. Just one spoon. Thanks."

"Sure." The waitress flounced away.

"She seems a bit disappointed you're here with someone," Grace said on a small smile.

"Yeah, well, she's alone in her disappointment."

"Kind of you to say." Grace traced her thumb over the heel of Justin's hand, then opened her mouth and closed it.

"Something wrong?"

"What's going on here, Justin?"

"What do you mean?"

She tilted her head, gesturing to the café. "This."

"Shockingly, people are eating." He leaned forward. "And we're going to join them."

Huffing, she shook her head. "That's not what I meant and you know it."

Justin didn't let go of her hands. Instead, he waited to speak until she looked at him. "We're finally sitting in a restaurant holding hands and sharing a meal, no ethics clauses clouding the view. We're exploring what might happen when everything else is peeled away and it's just us."

Her breath caught and her fingers tightened around his. "And what might happen?"

"Whatever we both consent to. Nothing more. Nothing less."

"I'm not going to be in Seattle much longer, Justin. I don't want serious. All I want is to…play."

Grinning at her, he shook his head. "You have a thing for board games?"

"Not until about thirty minutes ago."

Ignoring the disapproving glances, he leaned over the table and kissed her gently before settling back in his chair. "Which piece do you want to be?"

"All of them, and more than once."

Her husky answer wound him up. Lust and longing and sexual hunger created a volatile cocktail of need that swam through him. "I promise you'll pass 'Go' more than once."

She grinned and shook her head. "I can't believe we're sitting here sexing up an eighty-year-old board game."

"And I find it strangely attractive that you know how old the game is."

"One of my useless pieces of trivia gleaned from years of…" She trailed off.

"Years of what?" he pressed.

She took a moment to meet his gaze. "Just a lot of lonely years."

The waitress slid his sandwich on the table and refilled their drinks before leaving.

"Want a bite?" Justin asked, taking his hand away from hers to pick up the sandwich.

She shook her head as if to clear it. "No, thanks."

"Ah. Holding out for dessert. I knew you were my kind of woman."

"We'll see about that." She reached over and took a fry. "They're hot."

"Consider me forewarned," he said softly.

Her eyes darkened. "How in the hell did you just make a single french fry sexy?"

"Sweetheart, I didn't. *You* did." He took a bite of the sandwich and chewed slowly, watching her.

"You're killing me, Smalls."

He paused, sandwich halfway to his mouth. "You're a fan of *The Sandlot*?"

"You just earned major points for actually recognizing where that quote comes from."

"What about you?"

She shrugged, pushing her hair over her shoulder. "My mom wasn't the most involved mother. I grew up believing *Scooby-Doo* was the evening news, and if I could find a book to lose myself in? Well, that was the best of all. You'll be stunned to learn I've been a pirate, a mercenary, a vampire, a steampunk inventor and, on more than one occasion, a damsel in distress."

He licked salt off his finger. "You don't strike me as distressed."

"No, I'm not." She shrugged. "I've never been that woman."

"Want to know my other favorite quote from that movie?

'Anyone who wants to be a can't-hack-it pantywaist who wears their mama's bra, raise your hand.'"

She laughed. "I forgot about that one!"

The sound of her laughter slid through him like some kind of chemical reaction, pulverizing common sense until he was nothing but a mass of desire. "Grace," he said, choked.

Watching him, she reached over and slid the plate away and flagged the waitress. "Can we get our dessert?"

"Was there something wrong with your sandwich?" the young girl asked.

"No," Grace answered. "We're just anxious to share dessert."

"Very anxious," Justin quietly added.

The waitress rolled her eyes but took the half-eaten sandwich away.

Lacing their fingers together, he was surprised at how small her hand seemed in his.

"Justin?"

He met her stare, letting everything he felt show in his eyes. "Every time you came into class, every time you stopped by my office with research notes or questions on theory or treatment options, every time we ran into each other on campus—I knew you were smarter and more driven than any of the other students. You were special. There were obstacles, boundaries I wasn't willing to push. Those are gone. I want you."

The waitress set the crème brûlée between them. "Enjoy."

Justin didn't let go of Grace's hand. Instead, he picked up the spoon with his free hand and scooped up a small bit of the creamy dessert and held it out. "Bite." A statement, not a question.

She complied without any hesitation, her lips closing over the spoon, her eyes fluttering shut in absolute bliss.

A rush of heat flooded his groin, and his cock kicked against his jeans.

"That's delicious," she murmured, licking her lips.

He leaned over and tasted the sweetness from her mouth.

Her eyes flared before closing again.

She tasted decadent, rich and smooth with a hint of crisp, caramelized sugar.

It was the best taste he'd ever had on his tongue.

Taking the spoon from him, she set it down and retrieved a strawberry. She presented the meatiest part of the fruit, tracing his lips with it, teasing, before she let him take a bite.

Justin realized he was going to cause a scene when he stood up and the world caught sight of the undeniable erection pounding against the waistband of his jeans.

"Jeez. Get a room," someone nearby muttered.

Annoyed someone would disrespect Grace, he started to whip around and address the speaker.

Grace squeezed his fingers, stopping him.

"That's a fabulous idea," she said, so softly he thought he must have misunderstood.

"Sorry?"

She met his gaze without flinching. "I said, that's a fabulous idea."

"Getting a room?" he asked stupidly.

"Yes, Justin." She leaned over and nipped his bottom lip before whispering, "And make it somewhere nearby."

He let go of her hand to flip the check over as he dug out his wallet. He dropped enough to cover the bill and tip, grabbed Grace's hand and hauled her out of the restaurant.

She laughed as she followed. "It doesn't have to be a fifty-yard dash."

Opening the car door for her, he muttered, "The first time, it probably will be. After that? Monopoly is all about strategy and longevity, baby." He met her wide-eyed gaze. "This is what you're getting into with me—all night. No compromises on pleasure given or received. No apologies tomorrow. We talk about what happens next after that."

"Take me to breakfast and you've got a deal."

"Done."

Justin did his best to walk to the driver's side calmly. He was pretty sure he failed.

JUSTIN WAS ALREADY backing the car out of the parking space before Grace could buckle her seat belt.

He sped down the 519, his eyes scanning the buildings as they flashed by. "If you don't have any objections, I thought the Best Western in Pioneer Square would be nice."

"Sounds perfect to me," she said, voice husky.

Justin's grip tightened on the wheel as he sped up. "You're making me crazy. The voice thing? It's going to push me over the edge."

"Can't help it," she murmured.

He glanced at her quickly. "Seriously?"

"Happens when I get turned on, I guess."

"You guess?"

"It's never happened before."

"Why now?"

She laughed. "You seduced me, Justin. From the moment you stood in front of me at the club to the strawberry kiss, you…you… Yeah. You seduced me."

His jaw tightened. "I haven't talked you into anything you don't want to do, have I?"

"Considering this is a mutual agreement, there's been no 'talking me into' anything."

He stepped on the brakes hard and whipped the car into a narrow space in front of the hotel. "Wait here. I'll get a room."

She reached for her purse. "Do you want me to pitch in half?"

"Hell, no. Just be here when I get back and we'll call it even."

"Justin?"

"Yeah?"

"I'm going to head in and wander around."

"Why?"

Her grin was pure sex. "So you can find me."

His mouth went drier than if he'd filled it with Pixy Stix candy. Nodding, he pushed off the car and jogged into the lobby only to end up waiting in line behind a pissy traveler. Nothing about the guy's requests was possible, and Justin grew more and more agitated as he waited. She walked past him and his gaze locked on her.

Calm just wasn't in his repertoire at this point. He had to get this first rush of Grace out of his system. Then he could slow down and enjoy the night. Until then, he was going to burn for the woman who was at this very moment peeling an orange from the breakfast area and waiting on the elevator to go who-knew-where.

Something about that challenge, to hunt her down, claim her as his prize, made him want to shove the stranger in front of him aside and demand the first available room with a king-size bed.

When the guy in front of him finally stormed off, Justin stepped up to the counter and pulled his wallet out. "I need a room for two, king bed."

The sleepy-eyed clerk didn't even glance up from the computer. "Smoking or nonsmoking?"

"Non."

"Floor preference."

"First available."

"Front or rear of the building."

"Look," Justin said, leaning over the counter. "Give me

a room with a king-size bed that's clean and has room-darkening drapes in this zip code and I'm cool. Just get me the key before I rupture a nut, feel me?"

A lazy smile spread across the guy's face. "Saw you two come in. She's hot as hell."

"Then have a little sympathy, man. A key."

"Cash or credit?"

"Cash plus a tip if you'll just give me the damn key," Justin all but snarled.

A couple of taps of the keyboard and the clerk produced two key cards.

Justin paid him in ones and fives, not thinking about it until the guy arched a brow.

"You pick her up at a strip club?"

"Yeah."

"Cool. Where does she work?"

"Man, she's not the stripper. *I am.*" He scooped up his wallet and glared at the guy. "Good night."

"Not as good as yours is gonna be," the guy muttered, shifting to stare at the computer again.

Justin didn't comment, didn't spare the guy another look. He went straight to the car and parked it near the first exterior entrance. The room number put them on the fourth floor. He'd start on the second floor and sweep every hallway until he found her. And when he did? He was passing Go and collecting his two hundred dollars.

Immediately.

GRACE WANDERED ALONG the third-floor hallway, slipping into every vending nook and laundry cranny as she waited for Justin. No telling what was taking so long. The thought that he'd changed his mind and bailed on her flitted through her mind before she dismissed it. He wasn't the type to go back on his word. She knew that much about him.

A stairwell door closed heavily behind her.

Strong hands spun her around and yanked her into a hard body before she had a chance to react. "You don't hide very well, Ms. Cooper."

Her breath hitched. "Maybe I wanted to be found, Dr. Maxwell."

"Did you now?" he murmured.

"I bit my lip when you pulled me around." His mouth was so close to hers their lips brushed, featherlight, as she spoke.

"I apologize."

"Don't." Her pulse thundered. "Kiss it and make it better."

Tipping her chin up, he closed the distance between them. Their lips slid together like two puzzle pieces clicking into place, solid and secure. Tongues touched, tentative before growing bolder. Hands roamed, slow but desperate. And in no time at all, she was lost to the moment.

He treated her like a sensual feast, caressing her face, her neck, the upper swells of her breasts. His short breaths skated over her skin. When he slipped a hand under her shirt and found one nipple, she gasped his name and let her head fall against the wall he pinned her to.

Those magic fingers disappeared seconds before he pulled her close with one hand and cupped the nape of her neck with the other to direct the kiss.

Hunger. He made her hunger for him. Deprived of such sensual sensation for so long, she couldn't do anything more than follow his lead in the moment. She knew she needed to get her feet underneath her, regain control, and she would. Grace might be a lot of things, but out of control wasn't one of them.

As if he'd heard her, he broke the kiss. He stared down at her, his blue eyes darkened with lust, the pupils dilated. "C'mon."

Justin ushered her into the dimly lit stairwell and jogged up the stairs, hauling her along. He emerged on the fourth floor, went to room 420 and, with a shaking hand, inserted the key card. The electronic lock clicked open and he pulled her into the dark room, this time letting the door shut quietly behind them. The moment they were inside, he had her pressed into the corner and slipped his hands up under her shirt to unhook her bra with deft fingers. When the clasp released, he moved to cup one bare breast. The nipple, beaded before he reached it, hardened even more as he pinched and tugged the tender flesh.

Grace slid her hands under his coat, around his waist and up his shirt. Skin to skin. Heat to heat. She reveled in his shudder when she raked her fingernails down his spine, grew empowered by his increasingly frenzied actions. Never in all her life had she felt so raw. When he bent, wrapped his arms around her waist and hoisted her against the wall, her legs automatically wrapped around him and her hips thrust forward.

Justin settled the seam of her sex against the hard ridge of his erection and ground into her.

She gasped and arched her back, exposing her throat.

A primal growl built in his chest. He pressed his lips to her neck, alternately licking and nipping her jugular.

Grace wound her arms around his neck and rode his cock with growing urgency. Soft mewls filled the cool air, and it took her a moment to realize the sounds were hers.

He lifted her off of him and, despite her protests, spun her to face the wall. The button on her jeans made a soft *pop* when he yanked it free. Zipper teeth chattered their way down. He shoved her pants to her ankles. "Step out."

She did and, spreading her legs, arched into him. Her body came alive under his touch. Breasts heavy and core aching, she wanted him inside her. She craved him, needed him to stretch her and fill her and take her over the edge again and again.

The sound of a zipper was followed immediately by crinkling foil. Seconds later, the weighted heat of his cock settled against her ass even as unseen fingers slid over her hips and down.

"Sweet hell," he whispered into her ear as he worked his way into her folds. "You're so damn wet, baby."

"Please."

"I thought you wanted me to be the one to beg," he teased, tracing his tongue along the shell of her ear.

A desperate, choked laugh escaped her as she slapped her hands on the walls. "No more playing. Finish me, Justin. *Please.*"

Her slick arousal coated his fingers as he dragged them forward to the small, firm knot of her clitoris. Several short, swift flicks and she came apart in his arms.

Her hips bucked wildly, her breath came hard. Her eyelids slid closed. A deep keening escaped her. She shuddered, pulling a hand off the wall to clutch his and hold him closer as she rode out the crest of adrenaline and raw lust pounding through her veins, thick and viral. He scraped his teeth along the nape of her neck, sending her careening over the edge into a second brutally hard orgasm.

Nothing made sense for several minutes—not the thundering of her heart, not the sound of blood rushing through her ears, not the way her legs had gone to rubber. She was lost in space and time, nothing more than a product of her various pieces.

She was full and heavy, yet vacant, wanting.

She wanted him buried inside her, wanted him to drive her to abandon, wanted him to use her body well.

The images those thoughts conjured took her even higher, as did the knowledge it would all come to pass. She wouldn't have to fantasize about Justin Maxwell in the dark. Not tonight. Tonight the man was manifest, the fantasy a reality—and the reality was superseding anything her mind had dreamed up, whether in the light of day or the darkest reaches of night.

He calmed her, soothing her with words and fingertips and firm lips on sweaty skin. "That's one and two. Now turn around."

Her legs refused to cooperate. Hot hands closed on her bare hips and spun her, pressing her bare ass against the cold wall. "Justin," she said on a breath.

"Hold on, baby." His words were strained, heavy, full of his own sensual need. Grabbing her behind the thighs, he lifted her and pinned her to the wall with his weight.

The heat of his arousal branded her, left her gasping as she reached for him.

"Arms around my neck."

She complied.

He lifted her higher, tilting her hips to receive him.

The broad head of his cock breached her outer folds and she whimpered. "More, damn it!"

"I don't want to hurt you."

"Do it," she pleaded.

With one hard thrust, he seated himself to the hilt. His mouth crushed hers, swallowing her shout.

She'd known he was large, but being impaled by him was a whole different thing. Stretched farther than she would have guessed possible, pain and pleasure hovered together, shining bright and dark on ecstasy's horizon. Then he began to move with slow thrusts. Aching, heavy heat burned in her pelvis. Using his neck as a fulcrum, she pulled herself forward and nipped his ear. "Harder."

His groan vibrated through his chest and into hers.

She shivered.

Fingers dug into her hips. "Hold on, sweetheart."

He pistoned in and out of her with sheer strength, using

his hands to draw her off his shaft before driving home over and over.

Sweat slicked her hold on him as she tried to pull herself onto him even harder. "Please," she said on a moan. "I need…I need…"

His hand slipped between them and, as she rode him, found her clit. First contact nearly threw her off his length when she jerked, but he tightened his grip on her hip and set up a rapid thrumming in time with his thrusts.

In seconds, Grace felt the release roaring toward her. "Don't stop!"

"I'm with you, baby," he said on heavy breaths.

The spasm of orgasm started in her pelvis and spread. Then she came apart in his arms. Head thrown back, she took everything he had to give. Sensation overrode the last of her common sense and unintelligible sounds rose from her throat.

He sank his teeth into the soft spot between her shoulder and neck, and she reveled in the raw, animalistic behavior. Justin's entire body tensed and he groaned loudly as his thrusts became erratic. The pulse of his orgasm rolled through her. She reveled in the power of it, the power she wielded to make this beautiful man lose his control here, now.

The breath sawed in and out of her lungs even as her muscles went limp.

He pulled her free and let her slide down the wall until her feet hit the floor.

When her knees buckled, he caught her with his whole body, pressing her into the wall.

"Sorry," he murmured into her hair.

"You're apologizing?" Her gasp was lost to laughter.

"For mashing you against the wall. Nothing seems to be working right at the moment."

Fighting to regain her footing, she stood and wrapped

her arms around him. His jacket smelled faintly of his cologne, and she took a moment to close her eyes and bury
her face in that scent before sweeping up her pants.

"Drop the jeans, Ms. Cooper. I'm far from done with
you. Far, far from done."

Grace's belly fluttered in anticipation. Sliding her arms
around his waist, she gave in to the urge to snuggle in
closer.

He held her tight, whispering against the crown of her
head his intent to give her pleasure until the sun rose.

The raw power he wielded over her pushed her closer
to the edge of falling for Justin Maxwell—far closer than
was safe. But there was time enough to distance herself.
Tomorrow she'd let him down easy. Tomorrow…

4

HIS ASS AND ONE FOOT were cold. That was the first thought that went through Justin's sleep-addled mind before the click of the room's air conditioner further invaded his consciousness. *Air-conditioning is clicking instead of whining?* That meant he wasn't at home. One eye squinted open, fighting to focus on the alarm clock's huge red numbers—a few minutes after eight in the morning.

The mattress moved as his bed partner rolled over and stole more covers. He grunted softly as he pushed up to his elbows and turned to look at the tangle of curls spread across the pillow. In the dim light, her hair appeared dark. He knew that wasn't true. Grace's hair was actually almost brown until she stepped into the sun. Then it blazed like flame. A truer, deeper red than he'd ever seen anywhere else.

She was stretched out on her side of the king bed, her face sporting wrinkles from the pillowcase. Eyes acclimated to the dim light, he tucked a strand of her hair behind one ear and simply watched her. She was beautiful. Those cat-green eyes had expressed passion, reverence, humor and longing as they'd taken each other every way they could. Then, somewhere near six this morning, they'd fallen asleep tangled together.

He'd never had a night even similar to last night. Considering the remarkable quality of the woman at his side, he wondered if he'd ever have another. He had a real connection with Grace, something that transcended the physical. He didn't want to lose that, but he wasn't sure how to keep it, either.

No doubt they'd be going in different directions now that they'd both graduated. His focus was public service and hers was…what? She hadn't said. The money was in private practice. But even if that's what she pursued, it didn't necessarily mean she had to leave Seattle. She could find something here or at least nearby, and they could really see where this thing went.

Yes, he'd agreed last night was a one-time thing. And she'd made it abundantly clear she didn't expect anything more. But making more of this thing between them was the only way he could guarantee she didn't disappear. He'd spent years watching her, had finally found his way to her through dumb luck, and damn if he was willing to let her walk away because of the universe's poor timing.

He dragged a hand down his face and took a deep breath. They had cheered adulthood last night. Today it seemed more burden than boon.

"What's with the somber look?" Her voice, husky from sleep, made his breath catch.

"Just thinking."

"No thinking before coffee." She rolled closer to him and snuggled into his chest, slipping an arm around his waist. "It's a cosmic rule."

He stroked a hand down her hair. "Cover hogs don't get to make rules."

"I'm not a cover hog. I only took what I needed."

"That apparently equals everything."

She sniffed. "A girl has to have her standards." Her lips curled against his bare skin.

"Good to know." Rolling over, he pulled her with him

so she draped across his upper body. He was aware that he was holding her a little too tight, but he couldn't seem to let go.

"Justin?"

"No, no. It's fine. My most important body parts were only at risk of frostbite for a short while. They'll be fine."

She chuckled and propped herself up to meet his gaze. "If I wasn't sure it would lead to the crossroads of Wicked Lane and Wanton Drive, I'd offer to warm your most important body parts up."

His cock swelled. "Yeah?" He shifted against her hip. "I could get behind that."

She snorted. "You did."

The ribald reference to their lovemaking made him laugh. "You're a vixen, woman. A true vixen."

"Yeah. *Sports Illustrated* keeps calling for a cover shoot, but I'm just too busy being a bookworm. It's so much sexier."

"On you? Hell, yes, it is." Leaning in, he took her mouth in a swift kiss. "Your mind is definitely sexy. I loved watching you latch on to a concept or theory in class. Your brows would draw down and you'd get this look, as if you were so deep in your own thoughts you had no idea what was going on around you. I never knew what you'd say, whether you'd agree with me or disagree and defend your position so well I'd have to agree with *you*. I knew I'd never have to worry you'd play me false." He traced a finger down her neck and between her breasts, circling the lower side of one and watching the nipple pucker. "And for the record? Your body isn't half-bad, either." He dragged his gaze first to her mouth and then to her eyes. "Last night was awesome, Grace."

She shivered. "I was sitting here trying to come up with the smoothest way to say the same thing. But I can work with *awesome*."

Justin reached for a condom before he rolled over, blood flooding to his groin. "I'm headed down Wicked Lane. You take Wanton Drive. We'll meet at the crossroads."

Her lazy smile made his testicles draw up tight. "Wanton works for me."

He slid into her slowly, pausing when she winced. "Okay?"

"Just a little sore. That was a lot of mattress gymnastics for a girl who's gone more than two years between meets."

Cupping her face, he kissed her slowly before asking, "How long has it been?"

She closed her eyes, refusing to meet his gaze.

"Grace?"

"My master's program."

"You haven't been to bed with anyone in—"

"Twenty-seven months, Justin." She finally looked at him, her eyes hauntingly beautiful. "So, yeah. I'm a little sore." She slowly lifted her hips, drawing him in. "Doesn't mean I want you to stop."

So he didn't.

STEPPING OUT OF the shower an hour later, he heard his cell phone ringing. "Ignore it," he called out.

"I did."

He grinned and shook his head. Being with her was so easy, so comfortable. Part of him wanted to revel at how easy it was to like her as much as he did. Another part wanted to simply gather up his belongings and leave, ensure nothing could come of the spark harbored in his heart. The longer they were together, the more that spark was coaxed to burn. It scared him more than a little.

This time in his life was supposed to be about finding his professional footing, making a contribution to the Second Chances program and beginning to carve out respect from his peers. None of that included a woman, particularly a woman whose immediate future didn't align with his own.

He'd worked so hard to become the man he was now, not the kid in the too-small clothes, the one always looking to make money any way he had to in order to put food on the table. When his focus had shifted, when he'd begun to think in broader terms than street smarts and day-to-day survival, he'd found his purpose. God knew he hadn't been abstinent in the years that followed. He was no choirboy. But at the same time, a woman hadn't figured into his long-term plans.

And yet, he was fiercely attracted to Grace. She hadn't quite closed the door on a repeat of last night. Maybe he could see her again before they ultimately went their separate ways. And if their next time had to be their last time, he'd do his best to snuff out this burning desire he harbored for her, *had* harbored for her for the past three years.

Hands on the counter, he locked his elbows and leaned forward, head hanging loosely. He wanted Grace. Badly. Craved her, even. But the reality of their situation didn't change for his wanting her. She had a life to start and so did he. Their paths probably wouldn't cross again. His only chance was to press her for just a bit more of her now, while it was an option.

He finished brushing his teeth and stepped into the room, hand on the towel, and froze. Grace had opened the curtains just enough to peer out. Sunlight bathed her in a nimbus of brilliant gold, outlining every curve on her luscious, bare body.

Shifting, she offered him a partial profile and a wide smile. "Sun's out today."

"Good." The word was little more than a croak.

Her brows drew together. "Hey. Are you okay?" She started toward him and stopped when he backed up.

Justin couldn't think of anything beyond the woman.

Heart racing and palms sweating, he shook his head. "I'm fine."

"You seem a little shaky."

"I *am* a little shaky."

"Low blood sugar?"

"Yeah." Easy answer. A lie, which didn't sit well with him, but he didn't correct himself, didn't offer the truth.

How could he even be *thinking* of getting emotionally involved? She'd said she wasn't staying in Seattle long, but even if she was only here for another couple of weeks, they could see each other again He wanted to find out what might be between them, given time and a little nurturing, a little emotional excavation. "So…what's your next step, Grace?"

"What do you mean?"

"In life. You've graduated. What now?"

"You're standing there in a towel, I'm naked, and you want to talk career planning?" Her laughter rang out in the bedroom. "You're in a strange mood, Dr. Maxwell."

A twinge in his chest had him rubbing his left pec. "Admittedly strange."

"Okay, then. I have an eighty-hour job-shadowing practicum I have to complete. The college let me walk with my class at graduation, but I still have to get a passing grade on the practicum before I can implement my nefarious psychological practices on unsuspecting victims." She raised her arms, let her head fall back and loosed an evil cackle before bursting into laughter again. Dropping her arms, she shrugged. "So eighty hours of blah, blah, blah before I officially become a psychologist."

His chest tightened around the twinge. "Yeah? Are you staying local?"

She nodded. "Personal issues regarding my housing situation meant I had to stay close by."

"Want to have lunch, then, say, Wednesday? We can

meet somewhere midpoint for both of us." Postcoital meal arrangements might be backward, but it would assuage the guilt needling him for the screw-and-run he'd momentarily considered. This? This he could live with. Barely.

He'd take it.

A faint blush stole across her cheeks. "Lunch? That'd be great." The words were right, but the hesitation in them wasn't.

"Are you allergic to lunch?" he asked as casually as he could.

"No." She rubbed her throat, her free arm wrapping around her torso. "It's just…you remember I'm leaving right?"

"It's not a marriage proposal, Grace. It's just lunch."

She smiled up at him. "Okay, then. Downtown area would be easiest for me."

He exhaled slowly. "Excellent." They weren't through with each other.

Not by a long shot.

GRACE WATCHED JUSTIN'S shoulders sag and couldn't be sure if it was relief or disappointment. The former buoyed her while the latter stung like hell.

It shouldn't matter. She just had to get through the next two weeks and then she was following Meg to Baltimore where she'd try to find a job. It was as far as Grace could conceivably get from Seattle, her past and her mother.

Still, watching Justin's reaction was very much like holding on to a life vest in twenty-foot seas. A second to catch your breath before getting driven under again.

He squared his shoulders and crossed the room. "How about Tuesday? I don't want to wait until Wednesday." Cupping her face, he leaned in. "Say yes." The smell of minty toothpaste on his breath combined with the scent of the hotel's soap and shampoo on his skin to form a clean smell she knew she'd never forget.

"Yes."

"And dinner with me Wednesday."

"Yes." The answer was out of her mouth before she truly considered the implications.

"Good." He closed the distance and kissed her, lips soft yet firm as he laid claim to her mouth, owning the moment, owning her, in a way that disconcerted her. No one had ever made the effort to get to know her, to see her, to invest in her. Then Justin happened.

It was only supposed to have been one night. Not a date. No expectations. Nothing more. But he'd been so sincere in his interest, so transparent in his desire for her. What woman wouldn't want to enjoy that for just a bit longer?

He'd caused her to reconsider everything she'd thought would be true today. And she wasn't sure how to revise her expectations because he'd left them open-ended. Living with a "maybe" where Justin was concerned was dangerous. She needed concretes, absolutes, not maybes and what-ifs. She could manage this…this…*fling* if she kept it in perspective. Because while his invitations certainly changed the rules they'd established, the outcome was pre-determined and non-negotiable.

She wouldn't allow him to derail her goals, professional or personal, no matter how long she'd wanted just what he offered right now. She'd worked too hard, made too many sacrifices to let it fall apart now because of a man… no matter how much she might want said man. With autonomy would come more opportunity, but as long as she was in Seattle? She'd always be Cindy Cooper's daughter, the runt who couldn't get out of the woman's way fast enough. Grace refused to live in that emotionally putrid place anymore.

She wouldn't allow one night with Justin to potentially

change everything she thought about her career, her future, her*self*.

Feeling her stiffen in his embrace, he broke the kiss and, still cradling her jaw in those large, capable hands, rested his forehead against hers. "Stop overthinking things."

"Stop reading my face."

"Stop projecting every thought you're having."

She rolled her forehead back and forth against his.

"Seriously, Grace. Stop borrowing tomorrow's trouble. Today has plenty of its own."

"Stop sounding like a fortune cookie." She paused and rolled her eyes up to meet his stare. "Unless you've got the winning lottery numbers printed on your body. Then, by all means, proceed."

He grinned, the tiny crow's feet at the corner of his eyes apparent this close. "You can check it out if you want."

"Cute. We've got to get out of here in the next half hour."

"Let's hurry and get breakfast."

"Sure." She waited. He didn't move. "You have to let go of my face first."

Quick and hard, he took her mouth, backing her up against the wall as he kissed her.

When he shifted and let his lips trail down her neck to nip her collarbone, she shivered. "You have a real thing for walls."

"Not until you, I didn't."

The hummingbirds in her belly took up acrobatic maneuvers, successfully avoiding her pride's attempts to squash them. She couldn't help it if he kept saying all the right things. Every woman wanted to know she was wanted.

Wanted.

The idea she could be part of something bigger than just herself, that she could spend the next two weeks with someone, with *him*, was the greatest temptation she'd faced in, well, ever. She'd spent a lifetime alone, craving the things her friends took for granted—parents, extended family, the dreaded Christmas sweater, conflict between Aunt Jane and Uncle John. College had alleviated some of that when she'd met her three closest friends, but there was still a longing for family she didn't dare look at too closely. It would simply remind her that her past hadn't taught her anything about what it was to love or be loved. That was a reminder she neither wanted nor needed.

With Justin, she could have a short window of belonging. Granted, it wouldn't be forever, but it would be for now, and that was far more than she'd thought to get out of a one-night stand. She'd just have to make sure she kept things lighthearted so no one got hurt when she said goodbye. What could possibly happen in two weeks that would change the ultimate ending?

The answer was easy. Nothing would happen that she didn't expressly allow.

Decision made, she wove her hands through Justin's hair and pulled his mouth back to hers, seizing control of the moment. Their tongues sparred against one another, wrestling for dominance.

He groaned, grinding his towel-clad hips against her. Planting a hand on the wall beside her head, he broke the kiss, resting his chin on her head. "You're going to make me miss the hotel's free waffles."

"They're overrated."

"Had them before?"

"Nope, but I've had you. How can a measly fast-food breakfast hold up to the Mighty Maxwell?"

His bark of laughter surprised her. "You're quick. I'll give you that. And your flattery will ensure you get the first 'measly' waffle."

"Your priorities are messed up," she muttered, ducking under his arm and gathering her clothes.

"There's still lunch—and dinner—later this week. You agreed. I promise dessert will make up for today's disappointment."

"It better. I want pie this time. *Good* pie."

His lips twitched. "I can manage that."

"Huh." She pulled on her thong. Jeans followed, then her oxford, wrinkled as it was. Her shoes proved elusive, and it took her several minutes to find them—one in the bathroom and the other in the closet. Go figure. Hopping on one foot, she absently called through the room to Justin, "So, what have you got going on this week?"

"I start my new job tomorrow."

"Yeah?" She slipped into the bathroom to try to wrangle her hair into some form of submission. "Hand me my purse, would you?"

He set it on the counter before he went back to putting himself together.

She dug through her bag, finding a hair tie and a small brush. *Score.* A ponytail would work. Slowly working out the knots was a trial in absolute patience. "So, what are you going to be doing?"

"Working for a nonprofit that helps disadvantaged youth."

Her heart stalled as a block of ice landed in her belly. "Yeah?" She tried for a nonchalant tone but hit somewhere closer to high-pitched curiosity.

"Yeah. Great place. They were a huge part of my life years ago. I wouldn't have gone to college let alone pursued my doctorate if it hadn't been for their program."

"Yeah?" she asked again, fumbling the brush. It clattered to the floor, the sound seemingly amplified by her anxiety. "So, what's the name of this place?"

"Second Chances." He stepped into the bathroom and

sat on the tub's edge to tie his boots. "Pretty appropriate name, actually. It's exactly what they offer kids who—" He glanced up, brow furrowing. "What's the matter?"

"Well, this is awkward." She tried to swallow, but her throat had apparently mummified.

"What?" When she didn't answer, he set his foot on the floor. "What is it?"

The ominous tone of his voice said he knew but didn't want to accept the truth. Too damn bad. There wasn't an easy way to change what she had to say.

He stood, looming over her.

She crossed her arms under her breasts.

"Shit." He raked his fingers through his hair.

"Pretty much."

"Why didn't you mention you were doing your practicum at Second Chances?"

"I could ask you why you didn't tell me you would be working there. Same answer, Captain Obvious. I had no idea it was relevant."

He stalked out of the bathroom and, if she interpreted the sound correctly, punched a pillow before his words punched the air. "Freaking fabulous."

"You know what? You better gain a little perspective and a lot of control, fast. You're acting like I did something wrong. News flash—I didn't. So get over yourself and cut the temper-tantrum crap."

"Grace, if they find out I screwed around with an intern, I could be fired before I even start. This could destroy my career. Don't you get it? You may have just ruined my life!"

How often had she heard the very same thing from her mother? How often had she been forced to listen to all the things her mother would have seen and done if she'd been able to afford an abortion?

"Go to hell," she whispered, the words a gauntlet thrown

down after a lifetime of blanket neglect and emotional abuse.

Snatching her jacket off the luggage rack, she blindly dug out a handful of bills and walked over to Justin, dumping them at his feet. "Here's the tip I didn't give you last night, and some free advice, too. Never piss your 'client' off before you've been paid or the deal might fall through."

His eyes narrowed. "Did you just call me a whore?"

"I'm losing my touch if you have to ask." With that, she headed toward the door. "Enjoy your waffles."

5

JUSTIN HOPPED OFF the 28 bus and, shoulders hunched, started up the sidewalk. Though it was only a couple of blocks to his mom's, the walk through this neighborhood could be a little dicey. The area was rough, but it wasn't particularly violent during the day. That didn't mean it couldn't be under the right circumstances, though.

Levi had offered to drop him off when Justin had returned the car, but he wanted time to think before he walked through into his childhood home for the traditional Sunday supper. He knew his family would sense his mood and ask him what was wrong. He wasn't quite ready to answer those questions. Not with Grace's fresh, clean scent still flooding his nose and those accusing green eyes filling his mind. It was hard to piece together exactly how they'd ended up exchanging such vitriolic words and letting something with so much potential go up in spectacular flames.

It was the worst possible reminder of who he'd been— the kid with potential who never quite got it right. Was he still that same kid? Would he never outgrow the impulses that led him to screw things up just when the perfect opportunity presented itself? Would he never be able to hold his damn tongue when someone seriously pissed him off?

If he couldn't manage these basic human decencies, he was destined to fail at whatever he tried to do or be.

Justin strode up the front walk as he had a thousand times before. Sounds from the television leaked through ancient caulking around the windows, and the CBS Sunday-morning news anchor's distinctive voice was followed by dramatic music and a second reporter's voice. The front door stuck when Justin twisted the knob, forcing him to put his shoulder into it. He'd have to fix that. The last thing his mom needed was having to muscle open the door after she'd been on her feet for ten straight hours, waiting tables all night.

"That you, baby boy?" she called from the kitchen.

"Nope." *Crap, the kitchen.* Yep. She was going to want to talk. Not yet, not yet, not y—

"Step into my office, sweetheart."

Resigned, he dumped his messenger bag on the sofa. The smells of lemon oil and fabric softener were subtle but pervasive, clean scents that comforted him. Pausing in the doorway, he watched as his mom made coffee with absolute economy of motion. She still wore her black pants and white shirt from the diner, but she'd exchanged her sneakers for slippers. *Such a beautiful woman,* he thought. *Such a hard life.* But it had been that way for all of them after his old man had been killed sixteen years ago, and he hadn't made it any easier by finding ways to express his grief through a life half-lived on the streets.

Glancing over her shoulder, she tipped her chin toward the table. "I watched you walk up—one of those nights at the club, hmm? Have a seat, even though you didn't call to let me know you were coming today."

He slid into his chair and balanced on the two rear legs, hands crossed over his belly. "I don't think my forgetting to call in for Sunday supper reservations constitutes a kitchen inquisition, does it?"

"Depends on whether or not you make me break out the thumb screws."

"Funny lady." She set a cup of coffee in front of him, the color a deep caramel, and he sighed. "You know, I'll be certain I've found the woman for me when she can make coffee as well as you can." He lifted the mug to his lips and, at the same time, they both said, "Dollop of love."

Laughing, she pulled up a seat. "So, what happened?"

"Club was fine. Then I had a…date. Typical kiss-the-girl stuff."

"Pretty story. Now tell me the truth."

Justin fought the urge to squirm. "No story. She's just a woman."

He hated the way her shoulders visibly relaxed, hated that he had caused her to fear he'd taken a huge step backward into his previous life of violence. Her fear was well warranted, though, seeing as he'd spent years putting it there.

"So, this woman. Who is she?"

"I'm pushing thirty-one, Mom. This obsession with my love life isn't natural."

"Your protest is duly noted. I still want to know who she is."

"Her name is Grace."

"Any chance this is the same Grace you mentioned a thousand times while you were teaching?"

"I beg your pardon," he answered, feigning indignation. "I hardly mentioned her at all."

"Justin."

He shifted to stare at the ceiling. "Yes, Mom. One and the same."

"Don't 'yes, Mom' me, Justin Alexander Maxwell. I have a reason for asking."

"You're nosy?" he quipped, wincing when she reached over and slapped his shoulder.

"Be respectful."

The sight of her settling in her chair, sipping coffee, equaled comfort. For all he teased her, he wouldn't give up these kitchen-table talks for anything. It was rare these days that they had a spare moment alone together given that his sisters always wanted to be involved in everything. He loved them, truly, but these quiet moments with his mother were precious.

Clearing his throat, he sat up. "So what's with the whole 'come into my web' business? You planning to cocoon me and drain my life force for not calling?"

"I ought to wash your mouth out with soap for being such a disrespectful brat," she teased, setting her coffee cup down and crossing her arms over her chest. Her face suddenly lost all traces of humor, and she stared at him with such intensity he wrapped his hands around his coffee mug to give them something to do besides fidget.

Unable to stand it, he asked, "Why are you looking at me like that?"

"You're avoiding the conversation. That typically means you've done something remarkably unwise and you aren't ready to discuss it yet."

His shoulders hunched. "Yeah, well, it would help a great deal if you didn't know me so well."

Leaning forward, she stilled his hands as he spun his coffee cup. "Talk to me, Justin. What happened?"

"Things that were supposed to be simple got very complicated."

"Complicated how?"

He whipped his chin to the side and popped his neck before sliding low in his chair. Settling back in his seat, he began twisting his cup around in his hands again, over and over, staring at the chip on the rim instead of looking at her. "Just complicated."

"Tell me one thing."

"Sure."

"Does she matter to you?"

"Jeez, Mom." Shoving out of his seat, he took the dregs of his coffee to the sink and dumped them out before rinsing the cup.

"Justin."

He faced her, propping his hip against the worn laminate counter and staring at her with as much detachment as he could muster.

"Enough said," she murmured softly.

"Nothing said," he countered.

"And that's enough." She stood, resting her hand on the back of the chair. "I'll be here if you want to discuss whatever went wrong."

"I just want to get on with my life, but it's not that simple." When she didn't press, Justin gently banged his head against the nearest cabinet door. "She's working with me, Mom. At Second Chances."

"That's a complication, but far from an insurmountable one."

He snorted. "She didn't tell me she was doing her practicum there. I wouldn't have messed around with her if I'd known. It could cost me my job. I can't afford that, not in the short or long term."

"Did you tell *her you* were working there?"

"No, but…" His mouth thinned as his jaw set, but damn if he could stop himself. "No."

"Then doesn't she have just as much right to be angry with you as you have to be angry with her?"

"She's just doing a practicum. This is my first professional job." He shoved his hands in his pockets. "It's not quite the same thing."

"Uh-huh. And why is that?"

"I have more to lose. If I'd known there was a potential ethical conflict, I would have kept my distance from her."

Darcy arched her brow. "You sound a bit superior there, son."

"Look. She's leaving after the eighty-hour investment. This is my job. I'll have to clean up whatever mess this causes, and that's if they even let me. I don't need the complication."

One corner of her mouth lifted. "I would wager she doesn't, either, Justin."

"You know how important this job is to me," he muttered.

"What I know is that you're sounding pretty self-righteous when you may well have done her as much harm as she's done you. Supper's on in an hour." When he started to respond, she held up a hand and walked out of the room.

As far as parting shots went, it was pretty damned impressive—she had managed to hit a bull's-eye over her shoulder.

She hadn't even broken her stride when she pulled the trigger.

GRACE SAT IN THE little crepe diner for the second time in twenty-four hours as she waited for Gretchen to pick her up. Taking the bus home had been an option, of course, but Grace had to return Gretch's cell phone before Gretch left for her new job in San Francisco anyway. But the moment she'd heard Gretchen's voice, she'd wanted the solid security of friendship, the only kind of relationship she'd learned to trust in and count on. Half the story had been out before Gretchen stopped her with a firm, "I'm on my way."

Grace dreaded the inquisition she knew she'd face when Gretchen arrived. There were things she didn't want to answer and things she couldn't. For example, Justin had heated her blood with a one-two punch of lust only to deliver a hard knockout that had left her cold. How was she supposed to explain that?

"See, it's complicated," she muttered to herself. "We had wild and crazy sex that blew my mind, but then this morning he became a self-righteous prick and blamed me for ruining his life."

Nope. She was going to leave that little nugget of information alone. There would be questions about his skill, about the whys and the hows of every action, and she couldn't relive it. No, that wasn't true. She couldn't *stop* reliving it. It was that she didn't want to share it. That, *that* was the sticking point in the retelling because she didn't want Gretchen to bad-mouth Justin in defense of Grace's own actions. It wouldn't be malicious. Gretchen would only speak out as a matter of loyalty. She understood that. But still…

Absently picking at a rough cuticle, Grace could admit to herself that she didn't want to be alone right now. She wanted to be reassured that someone had her back, and her friends were her surrogate family, the support she'd never had. They wouldn't let her suffer alone.

A gust of salt-laden wind whipped through the restaurant door. The breeze off the Puget Sound was cold this morning. Grace shivered.

Gretchen walked in followed by Lynn and Meg.

Gretch slid into an empty chair and flipped her keys around her pointer finger. Spin, catch. Spin, catch.

Meg and Lynn sat as well, each hanging their handbags on the backs of their chairs and covering them with their jackets.

Grace stared at her hands, picking at her cuticles. "Wow. The whole cavalry."

"Gretchen picked us up after you called." Meg laid her hand over Grace's, stilling the destructive habit. "This is the last time we'll all be together, so we thought we'd tackle this crisis as a group."

"I wanted to give your phone back, anyway." Digging the iPhone out of her bag, she slid it across the table to Gretchen, dismayed to realize her finger was bleeding. "Damn it." She sucked on the little wound and found it impossible to raise her eyes.

Gretch bumped her knee against Grace's leg. "We want to help."

"I get that." She blew out a breath. "I do. It's just a little raw." A second shiver wracked her. "I should probably have just taken the bus home."

Ignoring the last sentiment, Gretchen asked, "You cold?" She shrugged out of her jacket and draped it around Grace's shoulders, ever the maternal figure of the four of them.

Grace closed her eyes and took a deep breath before lifting her face and offering her friend a small smile. "A little, thanks." She wrapped the jacket tight, closing her eyes for a second.

What hurt the most was the fact she'd believed, even momentarily, that she'd meant something to Justin, been someone more than a passing fascination. He'd disabused her of *that* notion, that was for sure.

Lynn leaned close and rubbed one hand up and down Grace's arm. "You have to share details so we know whether to exalt him or duct tape him to a tree and deface any bare skin with permanent marker."

Grace tried not to smile and lost the battle. "You scare me a little."

"He's a stripper. Going up on stage with 'I suck in bed' and 'I smell like ass' written all over him in broad, black pen strokes won't make him any money." She sniffed. "And if that's not enough, just give me a few minutes. I'll come up with worse."

This time Grace did laugh. "No. Nothing worse." Winding her hands together, she fought the urge to blurt everything out, to tell them how much she'd felt cherished when she was with him, that he'd made her feel sexy, powerful and desirable in a way she never had before, and how much that mean to her. Yet when she opened her mouth, nothing came out.

"Grace?"

She looked up to find Gretchen's brows drawn. "Yeah?"

"I'm sure you don't need me to say this, but humor me, anyway. You shouldn't get involved with someone right now. Not seriously, anyway. You've got plans, sweetie. Dreams. *Big* dreams that don't involve Seattle or your childhood house or your mother's influence. You've fought so hard to be able to tell her to go to hell as you ride off into the sunset. Getting tied up with a stripper is going to mess that up"

"I know." Two words, so raw they scraped at her throat. She reached over and took Gretchen's hand. "You're right. Thank you for caring enough to say it out loud."

Lynn leaned her forearms on the table. "Okay, but he *is* a stripper. Surely you had some fun?"

Glancing at Lynn, she managed to smile. "Here's the deal. I'll give you one detail and then you let me sort out the rest before you grill me. Agreed?" She glanced from face to face.

"Agreed," Meg answered for the group.

Grace found it easier to smile than she would have thought. "He kisses like a mad god. Better than anything even you can imagine, Lynn."

"What do you—"

"Nope." Grace held up a hand, cutting the woman off. "Meg agreed on your behalf. No questions."

"Oh, damn. She did, didn't she?" Lynn leaned over

and jokingly tagged Meg. "You're demoted from group spokesperson."

Meg rubbed her shoulder. "I resign, you brute."

Gretchen stood. "Let's get out of here. We can talk on the way to Grace's mom's."

Grace opened her mouth to protest, as it was, technically, out of the way for Gretchen to drop her off first, but the other woman gave a minute shake of her head. She was giving Grace an emotional pardon. Once she was out of the car, the other two couldn't needle her, albeit good-naturedly, about her evening with Justin.

Nodding, she rewrapped the jacket around her shoulders. "Thanks, Gretch."

"No problem," she answered in a low voice. They headed to the take-out parking slot for the restaurant and Gretchen beeped the little coupe open before flipping the seat forward. "Rocky, you and your punching bag in the back. Grace in front since she's first out. Not to worry, though. There are still blows to be had. You two can spend the trip to her place fighting over who gets shotgun next."

Gretchen kept the dialogue moving all the way to Grace's place, regaling her with tales of other dancers from the night before. Meg blushingly owned up to buying a lap dance from Nick. Lynn started to razz her pretty hard until Meg retorted she'd only been brave enough to pay for the lap dance after watching Lynn on stage with a dancer named Derek. It went on that way between the three of them, the radio thumping out Top 40 tunes, until Grace found herself in the tiny driveway beside her house.

She crawled out of the low-slung coupe and helped Meg unfold from the backseat. "You guys try not to kill each other in Gretchen's car," she said in mock chastisement. "Blood's a bitch to get out of those pale interiors."

Meg laughed and waved her off before shutting the door

and rolling the window down. "You coming with us later to wander the shopping district?"

"I wish I could, but I really have to get ready for this practicum. You guys have fun." She leaned into the window and looked at Lynn. "When do you leave for Boston?"

Her friend made a sour face. "Tomorrow."

"If I don't see you, call me and let me know when you're settled. We'll catch up then."

"I promise."

"And then you're leaving for San Francisco Tuesday, Gretchen?" A small part of Grace's heart broke at the nodded affirmation.

"And I'm off to Baltimore Thursday," Meg added, closing out the departure schedule for the week. "You're still following me out in a couple of weeks, right?"

"Yeah. In the meantime, I'm being abandoned." Though she managed a light and teasing tone, Grace had to admit she really did seem that these women, women who understood her better than anyone else, were leaving her. It wasn't rational and she accepted it was part of life, but they'd been her surrogate family for over six years. They'd been her support system. They'd encouraged her when she'd needed it and kicked her ass when she'd needed that more. Without them, she wouldn't have graduated, let alone magna cum laude.

Emotion clogged her throat and she waved them off when they all began to talk at once. "If you don't quit, I'm going to start singing 'The Circle of Life' in my worst Elton John impersonation. We all accepted this would be one of many sucky factors in growing up." She swallowed hard. "It doesn't mean we'll grow apart, though. Now go. The song…it's coming on."

Offering a mock salute, Gretchen peeled out of the driveway. The women's laughter echoed as they drove away, and Grace was glad she'd been left with laughter instead of tears.

Grace started for the front door of the tiny house. Standing on the sidewalk in this neighborhood was as good as begging to be assaulted or shot. Sunshine wasn't a talisman against violence, particularly not here. It just meant targets were easier to spot.

Letting herself inside, she tried to ignore the smells of stale beer and old cigarettes that permeated the place. No matter how much she cleaned, she couldn't get rid of the pervasive odors.

"Just a couple more weeks," she murmured to the empty room. Once the internship was over, she'd be able to get out of here. She'd head to Baltimore, rejoin Meg and begin to figure out where she fit in the world. Thanks to Justin leaving things the way he had, there would be no ties to bind her to this place.

She couldn't wait.

6

HANDS TREMBLING SLIGHTLY, Justin retied his tie for the fourth time. The knot still wasn't right, but if he didn't leave now, he was going to miss his bus downtown. Being late on the first day of his new job would be a miserably epic fail—right up there with sleeping with the intern. Muttering a vile curse, he reached for the doorknob at the same moment his sister Evelyn pounded on the door.

"I've had to pee for twenty minutes, Justin. Face it. You're as pretty as you can make yourself without surgical intervention so come out already."

Why had he agreed to stay the night with his family? A cushy sofa and a good meal weren't worth this. He yanked the door open and scowled. "You're not the one running late."

"You wouldn't be late if you'd gotten up when your alarm went off."

"I *did* get up, but *someone* was already in the shower using up all the hot water."

"I couldn't sleep." She slid past him and into the bathroom. "Leave already. No one can stand you when you're in a mood."

"I'm not in a—"

Evelyn slammed the door in his face, clicking the lock in place with force. "Yeah, you are."

Irritated, Justin stalked to the sofa, dug out the only pair of oxfords he owned from his overnight bag, slipped them on and scanned the room. "Briefcase. Where the hell is my briefcase?" A quick search found it tucked behind the television stand. He jogged to the front door, surprised when his mother beat him there.

She smiled. "How could I send you off to your first day of work without wishing you well?" Looking him over, she nodded. "Don't you cut a fine image?"

"No pictures, Mom."

"You're no fun." On tiptoe, she gripped his shoulders and pulled him down for a quick kiss. "Knock 'em dead."

"I'll settle for grievous wounding on my first day."

"Glad to hear your nerves haven't killed your sense of humor."

"I really do have to go."

"You wouldn't be late if you'd given up preening twenty minutes ago," Evelyn shouted from the bathroom.

"Your day's only a couple of years off, child," Darcy called out.

"I'm leaving, Mom. I'm going home tonight, so don't wait dinner on me." He bussed his mom's cheek and was quickly out the door. He jogged down the sidewalk and caught the metro seconds before the driver closed the door. Inside, it was standing room only. Naturally. After two transfers and then three blocks on foot, he stood outside Second Chances with three minutes to spare. On a deep breath, he walked in.

The lobby smelled the same as it had fourteen years ago when he'd first walked through the doors to complete his community-service sentence. He'd been convicted of vandalism of public property, but only because the cops hadn't caught him earlier that night. Had they nicked him then, they'd have charged him with a hell of a lot more.

Relegating dark memories into the small mental compartment he kept just for that purpose, he squared his shoulders and forced himself to breathe slower. He wasn't that kid anymore and hadn't been for a long, long while. He'd proven it by taking the counselors' help in breaking free of his involvement in Deuce-8 as a messed up teen. He'd reinforced it by going to school. And starting now, he'd spend every day doing his best to make a difference in the lives of the kids who passed through the front doors. Second Chances. It was this place, and the people inside these walls, that had made the difference in his life. The biggest reason he was alive instead of a violent crime statistic lay in these halls, under this roof and on these grounds.

"May I help you?"

The feminine voice startled Justin, kicking him out of his Memory Lane waltz and landing him in the now. Years on stage at Beaux Hommes helped him put on his best smile as he faced the voice. "Justin Maxwell here to see Mark Sanders."

The woman—Mallory according to her name tag—stared for a full ten seconds before catching herself. "Mr. Sanders is expecting you, Dr. Maxwell. His office is down this first hallway, fifth door on the left. I'll buzz his assistant and let her know you're on your way."

Unease skittered along his spine. She'd stared so long he couldn't help but wonder if she'd ever been to the club, maybe recognized him as a dancer. He couldn't indulge his discomfort and worry about it now, though, and he sure as hell wasn't about to ask. That part of his life was, for all intents and purposes, nearly over. Trying to control his heart rate, he held out a hand. "Thanks, Mallory. I appreciate it."

She shook it, her grip limp, palm slightly sweaty. "You're welcome, Dr. Maxwell."

"Please, call me Justin."

She blushed and tucked her long, dark hair behind one ear. "Okay…Justin."

Nodding toward the director's office, he gave a small wave to Mallory and started down the hall.

Where was Grace?

The door to the office opened as he got there, and a short, balding man boldly took his measure. "Good to see you again, Dr. Maxwell."

"Just Justin, sir." For the second time in as many minutes, he offered his hand.

Sanders's grip was firm and dry. "A few things have changed since we first talked. Before we get into specifics, I'm going to send you to Human Resources to complete your new-employee paperwork and get your fingerprinting done. Should take about an hour. We don't have the luxury of putting you through a formal orientation process, so this'll have to suffice. Any questions, direct them to me." He gestured down the hall. "HR is the third door down. It's marked. Ask for Sharon. Have her paged if she's not in there. She'll set you to rights and then send you back here."

At the mention of changes, unease settled heavily in his gut. Surely his boss hadn't already found out about Justin's involvement with Grace?

One way to find out. "I'll admit I'm curious, sir."

"Nothing to worry about. Just a few personnel changes since you interviewed. See you back here as soon as you're done, son."

Surprise wasn't enough to temper the response that nearly choked Justin with unexpected emotion. He wasn't Sanders's son. He'd been that to one man and one man only, and that hadn't ended well. At all. To hide his reaction, he shoved his free hand in his pocket and clenched his briefcase tighter. "Yes, sir."

"Problem?" The question was posed civilly, but that didn't diminish the cool undertone.

"No, sir."

"We'll reconnect in about an hour, then. Don't let Sharon keep you longer than that. We're on a rather tight timeline today."

"Yes, sir."

Sanders opened his mouth to say something else, apparently reconsidered and instead sent Justin off with a nod.

Justin took slow, measured steps as he fought to regain control of himself. "Losing it on the first day over something so trivial is pointless," he said under his breath.

The HR department turned out to be one harried-looking woman behind a desk so covered in paperwork, Justin had to wonder how she kept from having regularly scheduled nervous breakdowns at ten, two and four each day. His face must have relayed his thoughts because she glanced up at him and smiled.

"You're Justin Maxwell."

"Yeah. You must be Sharon."

"I am, and from the expression on your face, I'd be willing to bet you wanted to add 'crazy' to my given name. Granted, crazy *should* be my name to work in HR."

"I'm just a little, uh, overwhelmed at the amount of paperwork you've got going on there."

"I'm purging old files so it's not as bad as it seems." She looked around. "That's a blatant lie. It's hell. It's every bit as bad as it looks. There are regulations for how long I have to keep every piece of paper, and no regulation is the same. Five years for one form, seven for another, infinity for yet others."

"How do you manage?"

"Don't make me try to rationalize it, Dr. Maxwell. If I do, I'll fail. Then I'll get up and walk out and probably be terrified to ever stop walking lest the forms catch up with me and murder me in my sleep."

"Fair enough." He stepped into the room just far enough to let the door fall shut behind him and, again, held out his hand. "It's nice to meet you."

"Same to you." She shook with one hand and with the other she dug through the nearest paper mountain, retrieving a thin file folder. "I've got a crap-ton of forms for you to fill out. Orientation will have to wait, so I haven't printed your employee handbook or the code of ethics for you yet. I'll try to get that done and bound today and leave it in your mailbox in the receptionist's office. No promises, though. It could be tomorrow." She looked around and sighed. "Or Wednesday."

"No worries. I have no intention of doing anything to get myself fired."

She smiled. "Great." Gesturing to a small table in the corner, she said, "Have a seat and fill out all the forms. I've highlighted the blanks you have to either fill in or sign. If you have questions, send a Sherpa to carry me away from this mountain of doom known as my desk and I'll happily help you out."

He laughed and some of the tension in his shoulders bled away. Paperwork he could handle.

It was the changes Sanders had hinted at that made Justin's heart race. He had no doubt one of those personnel changes would be Grace Cooper.

This program had pulled him off the streets when the choice was go straight or go home in a body bag. He couldn't lose this job because of one dumbass move. But there'd been so much potential between him and Grace. Could he stand to lose that?

For the first time since he'd blown up yesterday, he wasn't sure which loss would hurt him more—the job that meant everything to him or the woman who just might mean more.

GRACE SAT IN the lobby of Second Chances picking at a hangnail as she waited. She'd been a few minutes early, but that was better than being late for her first day. But her boss was behaving strangely, making her wait in the lobby for the past half hour. Whatever was keeping him busy seemed to take priority over her. Leaving her out here so long struck her as a bit unprofessional, though, even if she was just an intern. The man had been much more organized when she'd interviewed for the internship a month ago. Oh, well. No crime in being harried, she supposed.

Her gaze roamed the lobby and hallways again, dully noting nothing had changed since her last perusal.

Where was Justin?

A petite, dark-haired woman approached her and extended a hand. "Grace Cooper?"

Grace stood and shook the proffered hand. "I am."

"I'm Sharon Johnson, human resources director. I apologize for making you wait. You're not the only new employee we've got today."

Justin.

"I'm just a student, Ms. Johnson. An intern."

"You're being paid, right?"

"I didn't realize I would be, no."

"You will…for reasons I'll explain in a minute."

"Any pay is much appreciated," Grace said in a rush, and it was the absolute truth. She would stash every extra penny to fund the independence that hovered only twelve days away. This almost made having to live at home again, no matter how miserably short the time, worth it. Almost. She wasn't sure anything could make it entirely worth it. But the idea of a house that smelled of lemon oil and dryer sheets versus the stale stench of her mother's place fueled her motivation.

"Ms. Cooper?"

Grace jumped. "I'm sorry. What did you say?"

The other woman smiled gently. "If you'll come with me, we can get the majority of your paperwork done. As I mentioned, circumstances have changed, so the board felt it would be appropriate to pay you since you'll actually be sitting in on counseling sessions and writing up parallel case notes to the managing psychologist."

"I'll be seeing patients?" she squeaked.

"In tandem with our licensed psychologist, yes. It's my understanding you'll write up case notes for every session you participate in. At the end of your eighty hours, the managing counselor will write a letter recommending whether you pass or fail the practicum. The university determines the final passing or failing grade based on a sample of the case notes."

Grace's hand automatically pressed against her stomach. "Don't say fail. I can't afford to fail."

"I imagine you'll do just fine. Let's get that paperwork done so we can get you started, okay? You'll be paid at the end of your last day, so I have to get your information in the system as soon as possible."

"I'm your minion, Ms. Johnson. Where you go, I follow."

The woman laughed. "Nice. I just mentioned to someone I could use a minion. I think I referenced a Sherpa, though. Too bad you're not an HR intern. I could definitely use one right now."

"I couldn't do your job."

"And I couldn't do yours, Grace." She gestured down the hall. "I'm down here. Ignore the mess in my office. It's temporary."

They spent forty-five minutes going over the necessary forms. The entire process intimidated Grace. It wasn't that she'd never filled out the forms—she'd worked through high school and part of college. It was that this made her graduation very real. No longer was she a student working toward a diploma or degree. This job was the last thing that stood between her and autonomy, her and the real world, her and *life*. She could truly taste freedom for the first time, and she wanted it more than she'd ever wanted anything before.

As much as I want Justin? The unbidden question crashed into her hard enough she faltered in filling out her citizenship form, the pen skidding across the page. Acknowledging she wanted him but only now realizing how *much* she really wanted him shocked her. That she would compare him to her craving for independence blew a few mental fuses.

"Problem?"

Grace's head snapped up and a blush burned across her cheeks. "Yes. No. I mean, yes. I screwed up this form. Do you have another?" She closed her eyes and took a deep breath. "Sorry."

"No problem. I'll admit I'm curious what changed your signature into a random ink slash across the paper. You're sure you're okay?"

"Just an epiphany. You know, the kind that makes your hand convulse."

"I hate those." The woman handed Grace a clean form. "Better that it happened here than, say, on the road or something."

"No doubt." Grace started on the new form, chewing her bottom lip and belatedly realizing she was massacring her lip gloss. Forcing herself to stop, she met the other woman's frank stare. "Thanks for not pressing."

Ms. Johnson smiled. "It's not my place. Though I'm curious. In spite of the profession's reputation, I'm human."

Grace laughed. "You guys get a bad rap?"

"Human Resources is all too often not about the human but rather about the bottom dollar. It makes it hard to do what I want to do most, which is nurture our employees, or resources. But now I'm talking too much."

Tucking a loose curl behind one ear, Grace offered a small smile. "I have that effect on people."

"I suppose that means you're in the right career."

Grace found herself smiling. "I suppose it does." Finishing the last of the paperwork, she handed it to Ms. Johnson. "Where do I go now?"

"I'll take you to Mark's office. He wanted you to meet the psychologist you'll be working with."

"If you'll just point me in the right direction..." Grace's stomach did a lazy somersault. "It's very real all of the sudden."

"Let me reassure you that you won't have any trouble sitting in with this particular gentleman."

"Why is that?"

"I'm HR, Grace. I can't comment."

Grace's stomach took up a full gymnastic floor routine. "Good-looking, is he?"

The other woman's lips twitched. "You didn't hear it from me, right?"

"Minions never hear anything, Ms. Johnson," Grace said softly.

"Then let me just say you're going to be the envy of every woman in the place when they find out you're working directly with him."

Justin. It had to be Justin.

Grace pulled the office door open and peered out into the hall. Might as well get this over with. "Which office is Mark's?"

"Three doors down on the right. It's marked." Standing, Ms. Johnson held out her hand again. "It's been nice to meet you, Grace. Don't hesitate to call or stop by if you have any questions while you're here."

"Thank you. I will."

The hallway was eerily quiet so early in the day. The click of her high heels seemed preternaturally loud as the sound of each step ricocheted off the walls. Certain she was making enough noise to constitute herself a one-woman marching band, she went up on tiptoe to keep her heels from making contact with the floor tiles. She hesitated a moment outside the third office door, letting fear wash through her before summoning a tide of confidence to carry it away. Smoothing the skirt of her business suit and tugging down the jacket to ensure it was straight, she rested her hand on the door handle. "Show 'em what you've got, Grace Margaret Cooper."

With a small smile and a hell of a lot of bravado, Grace stepped through the door.

7

Justin was already in shock when Grace stepped into the room. He'd just been advised he'd begin seeing kids, *patients*, today—on his own. The woman who'd been scheduled to mentor him over his first thirty days had gone on emergency medical leave due to pregnancy complications late last week. That left Justin as the only counselor on staff.

Everything he'd learned over the past eight years vacated his brain. He couldn't even gather enough common sense to respond to Mark's basic introduction between him and Grace. He nodded at her.

Her face, initially open and pleasant, shut down.

All he registered was that his fingers had gone numb and he couldn't feel his feet. Not relevant to the conversation in any way, but that's where his head was in that moment.

"Justin?" The director's sharp address pulled him out of the mental fog.

"Sorry. You caught me at a bit of a bad moment. I apologize, Ms. Cooper."

A single, almost imperceptible tremor ran through her.

"I didn't mention Grace's last name, so I'm going to assume you two know each other?" Mark crossed his arms and leaned one hip against his desk, clearly waiting for someone to enlighten him.

Justin's heart nearly stopped. Giving his boss the truth was the only option, but the words were hard to produce. "Grace and I have a relationship outside of the office."

"No, sir," she interjected quickly. "We don't. We *had* a brief acquaintance. Nothing more." She glanced over at him. "And that was definitely over before we became coworkers."

This time Justin's heart *did* stop. For a second, he couldn't breathe. Black spots danced across his vision and his lungs gave up their push-pull partnership with air. "It's a relationship."

"I'm sorry you misinterpreted it as something other than what it actually was, Dr. Maxwell." She ignored him, focusing instead on Mark. "It won't impede our ability to work together, sir. What was and what is are two very separate things."

Mark considered her a moment before he spoke. "It seems Justin here doesn't agree."

Justin mutely shook his head while, internally, he was shouting at her that what they had was more than an acquaintance. She'd experienced more. He had no doubt she had.

But she'd also walked out on him. He'd let her go, an action that would haunt him forever. Unless he made it right. He opened his mouth to speak, but she interjected.

"I'm sure Dr. Maxwell is merely acknowledging that we share a common educational foundation. He's right, and I hope he agrees that this will allow us to work together well and serve the kids without any distractions."

"Very nice speech, Grace." Mark slid into his chair and laced his fingers together behind his head. "Now tell me what's really going on."

"I have to have this internship, Mr. Sanders. Without

it, I don't graduate and—" she spared a glance at Justin "—won't be able to get on with my life. I want to put in my eighty hours, obtain a fair grade and find my niche in the workplace. Dr. Maxwell has nothing to do with that."

"And what do you anticipate that niche to be?" he asked.

Justin tried to interject, but random hand actions were all he could offer. Neither Grace nor Mark paid him any attention. Sucking in a great lungful of air, he ran his hands through his hair. "Stop. Please, just stop."

Mark arched a single brow as he dipped his chin in Justin's direction. "He speaks."

"I'm understandably a bit overwhelmed. Between realizing I'll have patients immediately and then finding out I'll be assigned to conduct Grace's practicum, it simply took me a moment to process it all."

"I'll ask once, Justin, and I expect an honest answer." Mark stared at him over the top of his wire-rimmed glasses. "Is this going to be a problem?"

"No. It won't." *I hope.*

"Right answer. Your first patient is due in your office after lunch. Our IT guy is setting you up with an email address. As soon as it's functional, I'll send you your predecessor's notes. They might help. In the meantime, I suggest you two sort out how you'll handle the observation and case notes to satisfy the practicum. Your office is down the next hall, second door on the right."

Justin risked a glance at Grace. She was pale but stood straight, her eyes focused somewhere over Mark's chair. She lifted her chin and swallowed, offering a nod before pivoting to face Justin. The detachment in her gaze was like a dull knife carving out his heart. He wanted her to look at him the way she had that night in the café. He wanted her to smile and laugh and be the woman he'd... begun to fall for.

She was more, *they* were more, than a one-night stand,

no matter what she wanted to believe. If he had to lie to get through the moment and get her alone? Fine. He would. But the moment it was just the two of them? He was going to sort this insanity out and force her to acknowledge that he wasn't alone in this madness.

And he'd do it spectacularly.

"I'm not sure where I'll be working," Grace said unsteadily, shifting to face Mark.

"My office," Justin answered swiftly. "It will help with the case notes if we can discuss them and talk out any problems you have. You'll also be there if any kids or parents drop in. It'll be excellent exposure." *It will also keep you from running again.*

"Fine." She swept an arm toward the door. "After you."

"You two play nice." Mark stood. "And shut the door behind you," he called, picking up the phone. "Hey, Sharon. I just wanted to let you know—"

The heavy door clicked shut.

"Shit." Justin gripped the back of his neck and pulled until his arm shook. "He called HR to tell her there's a potential conflict of interest."

"There isn't a conflict, Justin." Grace's cool tone washed over him like an ice bath.

"There *is* a conflict, Grace, because—" He stopped speaking as they passed the receptionist's station. Smiling, he nodded at her and kept going.

"Already scoping out your next conquest?" Grace calmly asked.

Taking her arm, he steered her down the hall at a rapid clip. He stepped into his office and slammed the door, letting her go and rounding on her. "There is no 'conquest,' Grace." Chest heaving, he yanked at his tie. He couldn't breathe. "How the hell are we going to manage this?"

She crossed her arms over her chest and leaned against the desk edge. "There is no 'this' to manage."

"The hell there isn't," he said, voice low and fierce. "You walked out on me yesterday. You left before we could settle things."

"I figured ruining your life was a sufficiently dramatic scene between terminal lovers." She arched a brow. "Was I wrong? Would you have preferred more?"

"I'll admit my choice of words was poor, but—"

"Poor? Your choice of words was *poor*?" She planted her hands on the desk and leaned forward, eyes narrowed. "A poor choice of words is telling your gastroenterologist he has a shitty job. Advising the person you just spent the night sexing up that she's totally and completely ruined your life? That's a little beyond a poor choice of words, Justin. In fact, it's so far beyond the boundaries of poor choice I'd bet it's well into the land of the undeniably moronic."

He stared at her, caught between laughing at her examples and throttling her for not listening. Apologizing was hard enough.

"Do you get that?" she continued. "Do you understand what you said to me?" Her breath hitched, and she pressed her lips together so hard they nearly disappeared.

He lost the ability to speak as he realized that he'd hurt her. Deeply. Far more deeply than he had initially realized.

If life were fair, she'd refuse to have anything to do with him. Good thing he never counted on life being fair, because he was *not* letting this go. Particularly not now, not with her convinced she was a memory he could do without. He wasn't sure what she *was* exactly, but she certainly hadn't been a hardship.

First things first. If she was worried he'd be unfair in her practicum, he'd sort that out and put her mind at ease. He'd find somewhere she could gain solid, supervised experience with an objective psychologist. That would also free him up to actively pursue her and get her to admit that what was between them was greater than the sum of each of them individually, more important than the politics of higher education. He waved at a spare chair. "Have a seat."

Sitting, she crossed her long legs, her pencil skirt riding up her thighs and exposing more leg than his mind could manage.

Memories of the slide of that silky skin beneath his hands made his chest ache even as his fingers twitched. The smell of her perfume teased his nose. He had firsthand knowledge as to where, exactly, she dabbed it. His cock twitched.

"What?"

The soft question pulled him back into the moment. "Nothing." He adjusted the front of his trousers as surreptitiously as he could. No doubt she realized the truth given her slow blink and single shake of the head.

Reaching for the phone, he pulled his small Rolodex from graduate school out of his briefcase. He found the number he wanted and dialed. The phone rang three times before his former academic counselor picked up.

"Stephen Ramsey."

"Dr. Ramsey, it's Justin Maxwell."

"Dr. Maxwell now, isn't it?"

Justin couldn't stop the slow smile. "Yeah. I suppose it is."

"How's life in the real world treating you?"

"First day at the new job and I've got a professional problem."

GRACE STIFFENED. How insulting could this man be? *I've gone from ruining his life to being labeled a professional problem?* She started to stand.

Justin put his hand over the receiver. "Sit."

"Woof."

"Damn it, Grace. Let me fix this." He refocused on the call. "Right. I have a former student doing her practicum with me. She and I…" He propped his elbow on the desk and dropped his head in his hand. "It's not a desirable fit, Dr. Ramsey. What are the chances I could have her reassigned?" Whatever the man's response, Justin shook his head. "No. She has to have the final eighty-hour practicum to graduate." A pause. "Yes, sir. She's already walked with the spring class."

Grace sat there, adrenaline-fueled anger making her blood nearly boil. He was trying to have her reassigned. No discussion. No negotiation. Just *wham bam thank you, ma'am, find a new place to work so you don't screw up my life*. Maybe she wouldn't need the practicum because she was going to kill him. Dead. "No, sir. I'd rather not go into specifics. Let me just say I believe it would be in her best interest for someone else to mentor her." Justin paused. "No, sir. I'm capable, but—" He paused again, hand gripping the telephone receiver so tightly his knuckles bleached. "I understand. Thank you for your input."

Grace watched as he set the phone down with precision before slowly swiveling his chair around to face her. "We're stuck with this, Grace, so we're simply going to have to find a way to make the most of it. It's only ten days."

She glanced at the generic clock hanging on one wall. Two work weeks. Ten business days. Seventy-seven hours and eight minutes to spend with the man who had taken her higher and driven her lower than any man ever had. To watch the man whose mind she respected, whose body she coveted, whose smile she craved, as he helped people. "And if I quit?"

His eyes flared. "Don't even joke about that."

"If. I. Quit."

He sighed, scrubbing his hands over his face and muffling his answer. "You'd have to wait until next semester and apply for a new practicum."

Not an option. She had to get out of this town. She'd saved every dime from her work-study jobs, every extra dollar from scholarship monies and every penny she'd found on the sidewalk in order to have a tiny nest egg stashed for her move to Baltimore. She'd bought a few key wardrobe pieces for her job and had enough left to secure an efficiency apartment, set up utility deposits and stock her pantry, probably buy a decent bed. That was it. If she had to use it to re-enroll in school? No. It wasn't an option. He was right; they'd have to make it work.

Shrugging out of her blazer, she settled deeper into her seat. "So, how do you want to do this?"

He narrowed his gaze. "You couldn't manage to take five minutes to fight with me yesterday, but you're agreeing to stick this out?"

Her throat tightened, and she fought to swallow. "Yeah."

"Why?"

"If I ruined your life, you reminded me what was most important."

"And what's that?"

"Survival." The one-word answer was barely a whisper, but it scraped at her throat as if it had been shouted. When he looked at her quizzically, she shrugged one shoulder. If she spoke, her quavering voice and broken words would have given her away. She couldn't live with herself if she cried in front of him.

"Look, the best thing to do is to have you find another mentor who can give you an unbiased grade."

"Do you intend to fail me?"

"What? No!" He wove his fingers together, staring at them for several seconds before speaking. "No. I would give you whatever grade you earned."

"Then I'm staying." He opened his mouth, likely to protest, but she rushed forward. "What happened between us shouldn't have happened. I get that. But I can't afford another semester of school, Justin. I need to get a job, get the hell out of here. I can't do that without this practicum."

"It seems wrong to me."

"If you give a damn about anything but your own narcissistic drive to be viewed as pious and above reproach, you'll understand that letting me proceed here is what's best for me. Do you dispute the fact that part of the definition of right and wrong is fairness?"

"No."

"If that's true, do you believe it's fair to punish me, to make me put off my life for as long as six more months because you're mad?" She fought the urge to rub her clammy palms against her skirt.

"I'm mad you walked out on me. I'm not mad you're here." He closed his eyes and took a deep breath. "You didn't ruin my life."

"Words, once said, are out there. No do-overs. It's half the reason we have a job."

He chuckled, opening blue eyes filled with some emotion she didn't fully recognize. "You always couch the pain with humor?"

The truth slipped out before she could stop herself. "I'm afraid of what would happen if I didn't."

He cocked his head to one side. "What are you afraid of?"

She silently cursed herself. No way could she spell out for him her most basic fear. Behavioral conditioning—the theory that every behavior was learned—held that she might not be able to love because her childhood hadn't taught her loving behaviors. Was that true? Had her mother's choices doomed her to never experience love, to never give or receive it?

She fought to keep her breathing slow and even as her chest tightened and her lungs refused to work properly. No way was she pulling those questions out for his consideration, professional *or* personal.

Shaking her head, she laughed with intentional self-deprecation. "Oh, no. You're not using me as a warm-up evaluation. Dig around in your patients' heads, but leave my psyche alone. It's perfectly happy in its screwed up little world."

"I'm just curious."

"No, Justin. We aren't going there." She sighed, slouching in her chair and stretching her legs, ankles crossed.

"I want to understand you." He considered her long enough she fought not to squirm in her seat.

"There's nothing to understand. Seriously." She rolled her head back and forth, stretching her neck. "I'm simple and straightforward. What you see is what you get. Always."

"No pretention?"

"No." Her one-word answer was sharp and definitive. "I don't have any interest in that."

His gaze roamed over her body, lingering on her shoes. She'd found them at a second-hand shop, surprised to find the name-brand shoes in such good shape. Damn if she was going to admit she'd bought half of what she was wearing from thrift stores, though. It was none of his concern.

She crossed her legs with a seductive kick and leaned forward to glance at her shoes. "You seem to have a thing for my heels. Sorry. They're not your size."

He snorted, sliding lower in his chair and resting his hands over his abs. "I'm all about high heels."

The way his eyes sparkled made her grin despite her unwillingness to play this game with him. "Cute. And for the record, dressing well isn't pretentious. It's called job security, Dr. I-Wore-a-Suit-and-Tie."

One muscled shoulder lifted in a lazy shrug. "I didn't say anything."

"You didn't have to. Your eyes gave you away, cataloguing my outfit right down to my accessories."

"How do I fix this, Grace, this thing between us? Throw me a bone here."

She wasn't sure what to say. Even if she'd been confident, she didn't know if she could've come up with the right words, words that wouldn't have betrayed her miserably fragile state. Her gaze dropped to her lap and she fiddled with the hem of her skirt. "Don't do this, Justin. Not now."

"It has to be now. I can't spend the next two weeks side by side with you and not wonder what might be between us. I can't watch you walk out of here a week from Friday and not wonder what the hell I could've done, not wonder if I should've asked for forgiveness, apologized, or hell, even groveled."

"You hurt me," she whispered. "After one night you figured out the most damaging thing you could say to me, and then you said it. I'm not sure we can get over that."

"Don't punish me forever for my careless choice of words."

"I'm not punishing you. I'm protecting myself from the chance you meant everything you said."

"I didn't."

"Some part of you was certainly capable of articulating that you think the night between us was a mistake. I won't take the risk that that part is far more dominant than you realize."

"Grace—"

"No. Listen to me." One hand over the other, she gripped her wrists. "I don't owe you my history any more than you owe me your future." The lifetime of verbal abuse had never weighed more than it did in that moment, but she'd be damned if she'd share that with Justin. She didn't want his sympathy or his pity. "You're going to have to accept and respect that I have my reasons. That's not a negotiable factor, so there's nothing to discuss."

Pushing himself to sitting, he leaned forward and propped his forearms on his knees. His chin dipped to his chest. "How did we end up here, Grace?"

Silence stretched between them, heavy and somber.

The air conditioner kicked on, the vent's vibration creating a heavy percussion in the quiet office.

"Justin," she said at the same time he said, "Grace."

"You first," she insisted.

Lifting his face to hers, he gave a short nod. "How about lunch?"

"Lunch?" She glanced at the clock. Her stomach growled the second she realized it was noon. "I'm not sure it's a good idea that we—"

"It'll be quick because we have to be here and prepped for our first appointment in an hour and a half." He stood and offered her a hand.

Grace stood on her own and shrugged into her jacket. "Just lunch."

Fleeting disappointment shone in his eyes before he locked his reaction down. "Fine. As colleagues."

Dread and longing wrestled in her chest, bouncing off one lung and then the other with serious prejudice before they went into free fall. They snatched at various emotions on the way down and didn't stop until they hit the soles of her shoes. "Okay."

Justin opened the door. "After you."

Stepping through, her emotions crawled out of her high heels and came to rest behind her belly button. The tension singing through her said those battered feelings were prepared for full-blown, riot-gear-required anarchy. Her eyes watered with a particular emotion she wasn't willing to openly name.

She feared it might be regret.

8

NONE OF THIS was going the way Justin wanted. Not even close. Hearing the hitch in her voice, listening to the accusations in her words, witnessing the hurt in her eyes—it had thrown him. He hoped the hurt he'd caused was superficial. It was what lay underneath that wouldn't let him go, though. Below that painful veneer was a well of emotional damage she hadn't been able to hide. He didn't know who or what had caused it, though he intended to do his best to find out. The one thing he was sure of? She hadn't walked out on him yesterday. He'd driven her out that door. And the responsibility of his actions left him with the sensation he was sinking faster than a man wearing cement shoes in the Hudson.

There was only one thing to do. Starting now, he was going to seduce Grace. Not seduce her with suggestive dances or passionate kisses that would allow her to claim she'd only been caught up in the moment. No, he was going to offer small things, little words of kindness, gestures of comfort—whatever it took to get her to realize that he was a better man than he'd shown himself to be and that he hadn't meant what he'd said. She was smart. It wouldn't take long for her to put it together. He just had to figure out how to show her what Saturday night had meant to him. He figured lunch was a safe place to start.

Granted, it had been a spontaneous invitation, but it provided an immediate opportunity to start showing her who he really was, the man he'd become over the years, not the selfish punk he'd been.

"What do you feel like for lunch, Grace?"

The click of her heels on the old building's commercial tile was loud in the quiet hallway, and he heard the falter in her steps at the question.

She slowed. "I assumed you had somewhere in mind."

"Nope. I figured I'd leave that up to you."

"I'm not entirely familiar with the area, so I'll let you make the recommendation."

Well, this wasn't working out the way he had hoped, either. "Fast food or sit-down meal?"

"Anything that costs five bucks or less. That's what I've got on me at the moment."

A spontaneous idea rolled over him, and, instead of thinking it through, he simply went with it. "C'mon. If we catch the 12 bus, we'll have plenty of time."

"You didn't drive to work?"

"I borrowed the car from a friend Saturday night. I don't own one yet. Hopefully that changes in the next week." He stepped up his pace, not giving her the opportunity to question him further. His long legs ate up the floor and forced her to nearly jog to keep up with him.

She never faltered, never complained.

They managed to catch the bus, but only because they ran for it. All the seats were taken, so they grabbed the handholds above them and hung on as the bus lurched into traffic. Grace swayed, her breasts brushing against him. He closed his eyes for a second and managed not to groan. Barely.

"Sorry," she murmured, moving away.

The urge to lay his hand on the slight curve of her hip and keep her close overwhelmed him. He wanted to hold her against his body, tuck her up tight and breathe in her scent, experience the brush of her ass against him as the bus rocked to and fro over uneven roads. Clearing his throat, he offered her a small smile. "No problem."

She blushed and glanced away.

He gently hooked a finger under her chin and gently urged her face around to his. "Seriously. No problem."

"You promised lunch. *Just* lunch." Her voice was soft as velvet with an undertone of steel.

"I did. I didn't promise I wouldn't react to your touch."

"Then I won't touch you."

"My loss." He stepped back a fraction, ignoring the curious glances of those nearest them.

Her brows drew together as she peered up at him. She opened her mouth to say something when the prerecorded voice came over the sound system, announcing the next stop.

"This is us." He gave in to temptation and laid his hand at the indention of her waist and guided her forward.

She inched away. "I'm pretty sure I can find my way out of the bus, but thanks."

"Just trying to be courteous." And wasn't that a lie? He wanted to touch her any way the moment allowed, no matter that someone might witness the act. It was an innocent gesture that let him put his hands on her. He'd settle for that. For now.

"Thanks." Clearly discomfited, she stepped off the bus and moved aside to wait for him. "Where to?"

"Down this block. The diner is across that intersection," he said, pointing.

The short, narrow blue-white-and-chrome fifties-style diner was a landmark in the Capitol District. Situated on Broad Street and open twenty-four hours a day, it was always busy. The clientele was diverse, ranging from politicians to street sweepers. The food was amazing and kept all the patrons coming back for more. Justin would know. His mother worked there, and he'd essentially grown up in the place.

The idea his mother would meet Grace left him a little uneasy, but that was okay. He wanted Grace to realize that he was well aware of how to treat people, women in particular. He didn't like the fact that she seemed to consider him heartless. God knew he had been in the past.

Not that kid anymore.

The mantra interjected itself into his internal conversation. He'd learned to remind himself of the poor choices he'd left behind and the golden ring he'd dialed in and aimed for instead. He had his doctorate thanks to the Second Chances program and the woman Grace was about to meet.

He might be nervous, but he was also damn proud. His mother was amazing. He'd never brought a date to the diner—though he supposed this wasn't a date. If he had to ask for clarification, Grace would undoubtedly remind him it was "just lunch." Still, his mom would understand.

"Earth to Justin."

His gaze snapped to hers as they stood at the crosswalk. "Sorry. What was that?"

"How'd you find this place?"

"It's a bit of a landmark. The diner is owned and run by a cantankerous Irishman and staffed with the best waitresses in town. And if memory serves, I owe you a piece of pie. *Good* pie. There's none better than the chocolate cream they serve here."

She flushed, and her hand went to her throat. "You don't owe me anything."

"I pay my debts, and I say I owe you pie, so there you go. Pie it is."

The light changed, and they crossed the street, then the diner's parking lot.

Justin held open the door and ushered her inside. "Sit wherever you'll be most comfortable."

Hesitating briefly, she moved to a booth near one of the large windows and sat in the sunlight. It glinted off her hair, showing the deep reds and golds hidden in the dark depths. The light played across her face, warming the pale tones and making her skin nearly translucent. It lit up her eyes, making the green a bottomless pool of color. When she realized he was staring, she glanced away. "Let me be honest, okay? I have no idea why you wanted to take me to lunch. Maybe you're trying to assuage the guilt you're harboring over Saturday night or Sunday's words. Maybe you're trying to reestablish yourself as a nice guy. Maybe—"

"Enough," he said, quiet but firm as he slid into the booth across from her. "Stop it, Grace."

"Pardon me?"

"You heard me. Cut it out." He reached for a menu and slid it in front of her, fighting the urge to hunch his shoulders. She'd read him as easily as a freaking book. "I wanted to have lunch with you. You agreed to have lunch with me. That's enough." *For now.* "And while I might not be wining and dining you at the five-star level, the food's excellent all the same."

She frowned. "And the company?"

Eyeing the dessert case, his lips twitched before a sheepish grin spread across his face. "Actually, the worst thing on the menu might be better than the rancid company."

Her laughter rang out. "Duly noted."

The sound of her laughter whipped through him like a warm Chinook wind. He wanted to hear it again, would do almost anything to hear it again.

One of the waitresses walked by and winked at him, tilting her head toward Grace. That's when it hit him. Bringing Grace to the diner was tantamount to inviting her to dinner with his whole family, not just exposing her to his mother. The employees of the Broad Street Diner had been his family for more than fifteen years. They'd stepped in to rally round his mom and sisters after his dad had been killed. The waitresses had created babysitting schedules to watch his sisters when Justin had been so wrapped up in his own misery he'd been no help to his mom whatsoever. They'd pitched in to give the kids Christmas and birthday gifts. They'd donated extra shifts to simply help his mom make ends meet when they were all just as strapped as the Maxwell family was.

Familiar guilt at the choices he'd made long ago prickled along his nape. He hadn't been the best kid. Moments like this, moments when the past snuck up and surprised him, pissed him off. He'd paid for his self-centered behavior, rash decisions and darkest moments. Man, had he paid for it. No sense letting it crowd in on him now. He rubbed the tattoo that circled his left biceps, recalling the bite of the needle.

"Justin?"

His head snapped up.

"Your arm bugging you?"

"What? Oh. No. It's fine." He glanced over her head to find his mom chatting with a customer at the counter. He whistled softly.

She lifted her soft brown eyes from her customer. Those eyes wrinkled with her automatic smile and struck Justin silent. The soft depth of the crow's feet was new. Or was it? Had he just not noticed? When had she started to show her age?

"Justin!"

"Hey, Mom." The weight of Grace's wide-eyed stare slammed into him. Glancing over at her, one corner of his mouth kicked up. "Did I forget to mention my mom works here?"

TAKING A DEEP BREATH while silently promising herself she'd kill him slowly with a staple remover and a letter opener when they returned to the office, Grace stood and faced the diminutive woman with as much composure as she could muster. "Mrs. Maxwell? I'm Grace Cooper, a former student of your son's."

"It's lovely to meet you, Grace. Please, call me Darcy. Coffee? Hot tea? Soda?"

"Hot tea would be amazing." Grace was drawn in by Darcy's warmth and guileless smile.

Justin rose and followed his mom across the narrow aisle and around the counter, sweeping her into a huge bear hug. How such a tiny woman had birthed and raised the tall, muscular man left Grace completely flummoxed, particularly when he spun Darcy around, feet off the floor.

"Put me down, you big oaf."

"You wound me, Ma."

"I'll get my pie server and show you wounded." Darcy wiggled out of his arms. "Cream with your tea?" she asked Grace calmly as she tucked stray strands of hair into her chignon.

"Please."

"She gets 'would you like cream with that' and I get the boot?" Justin grabbed Darcy again and laid a loud kiss on her cheek. "I'm your son, Mom. Your *son*."

"You're a pain in the ass is what you are," she groused good-naturedly, slipping away to efficiently fill a mug with hot water and retrieve a tea bag. She spun away, moving swift and sure to pick up a called order, refill coffee mugs and set Grace's tea in front of her even as Justin returned to the booth.

Grace rolled the Earl Grey tea bag between her fingers. She hated Earl Grey but didn't have the guts to ask Darcy for something else. "You don't have to look at the menu?" she asked Justin.

"She'd only abuse me with it," Justin called over his shoulder before focusing his attention on Grace with a grin and shake of his head. "I've eaten everything on the menu at least once, so I'm familiar with all of it." He shuddered. "Even the meat loaf."

"My meat loaf's the best, kid," the cook called from the kitchen pass-through.

"Your meat loaf has lamb in it. Lamb does *not* go in meat loaf, Shamus."

"It does if you're Irish."

"I'm definitely more of, you know, a Fifth Avenue and Sycamore Street kind of guy."

"Still a smart-ass."

"*Always* a smart-ass," Darcy interceded, setting a cup of coffee in front of Justin before stroking a hand down his hair. "So how's the first day as Dr. Maxwell going?"

Justin answered and their banter continued as Grace stirred her tea, the diners' voices creating white noise for her rambling mind. She'd been stunned senseless the moment Justin whistled at Darcy. This little microuniverse could have come straight from one of her childhood daydreams, one where she'd grown up loved and cherished and part of a family. People looked forward to seeing her. She would have given anything to be part of this…this… soundstage. That's what this was. A soundstage. It left her waiting for the laugh track and cued commercial breaks.

How could this exist right in front of her and yet be so far out of reach?

"Grace?"

She blinked and raised her eyes to find Darcy standing over her.

"Your tea bag is coming apart, sweetheart."

"Right."

Darcy carried the cup away and returned with a fresh cup of hot water—and another Earl Grey tea bag.

"Thank you." Closing her eyes for a split second longer than a blink, Grace worked up the nerve to address Darcy. "What do you recommend today?"

"As if there's not a chalkboard special by the door," someone muttered behind her.

"Mind yourself, Mr. Kapps." Darcy's mild censure garnered an immediate apology. Nodding, she considered Grace. "We're famed for our burgers."

"And Shamus cuts a mean steak fry," Justin chimed in.

"Are you disparagin' my Irish roots, Justin?" the swarthy-faced man called through the pass-through.

"Your…Irish…roots," Justin hooted with laughter.

The cook blinked and then, apparently catching the play on words, laughed along with him.

Cue that missing laugh track.

"Oh, you two," Darcy sniffed, her merry gaze shifting to Grace. "Are you opposed to burgers?"

"I've been in college so long I've forgotten they could be anything other than the politically correct soybean patty."

Darcy clucked, tucking her pad and pen in one apron pocket. "Shamus, make the girl a bacon cheeseburger, extra fries." Grace didn't realize she'd massacred another tea bag until Darcy picked up the second cup. "Soda is more suited to a burger and fries than Earl Grey, which, for what it's worth, isn't my favorite, either."

Grace shot her a shy smile. "Thanks. Anything but diet is great."

"Coming right up." Darcy whirled away, all economy of motion and kind words as she worked her way along the counter, pausing to ring up a table of truckers heading out.

"Is she always like this?" Grace wondered if the ache in her soul translated through the emptiness of her voice.

"Like what?" Justin leaned around her to watch his mom. "A waitress or a mom?"

"Both."

"Yeah, she is. She never turns it off, particularly the mom part. It's why she's so popular here. People from all walks of life come in and wait for tables in her section." Pride shone in the son's words.

A mom.

Justin reached out and laid his hands over hers. "Is she that different than your mom?"

How had he once again managed to ask the one question that could shatter the illusion?

She tucked her hands in her lap under the table. "My mom?"

He settled in his seat and toyed with his straw as he watched her through pale blue eyes. "Yeah. What does she do?"

"She works at Glennmore Canning." *There. Nice and vague. Could be anything from the CEO to a janitor.*

"Okay."

The urge to ask why he'd just accept her answer nettled her, but she didn't want to encourage this particular avenue of discussion. Grace didn't lie about who she was or where she came from, but she also wasn't inclined to lay it out for dissection by someone who came from a veritable treasure trove of emotional riches. Sometimes it was wisest to simply stick to life's gray scale.

Picking at a cuticle, she fought to keep her voice level. "How'd you end up in psychology?"

"Long story." He shrugged as if to say, *Tit for tat.*

Glancing around to make sure Darcy wasn't nearby, Grace leaned forward. "What are we doing here, Justin? How is it I ruin your life but still warrant pie?"

He arched a brow and whispered, "We're eating lunch, Ms. Cooper. My understanding is that colleagues regularly eat lunch together. There's nothing nefarious in the offer that anyone, in the office or out, could find harm with."

"This isn't just lunch," she responded on a whisper.

"It's food in a diner at lunchtime, ergo it's lunch."

One corner of her mouth twitched. "Ergo?"

"Ergo. Now if you'll relax, I'll throw in that promised piece of my mom's famed pie for dessert."

"I have five dollars, Justin. The burger alone is going to be more than that."

"I've got it."

"No, you don't."

"I invited you out on Sunday—prior to our nuclear meltdown—and you agreed. We just changed the day. So relax. This was one of our prenegotiated items."

Caught completely off guard, Grace grinned. "Deal."

Justin reached over and tucked a strand of hair behind one ear. "Deal," he repeated softly.

"Burgers are up, Darcy," Shamus called.

And Grace couldn't help but wonder what, exactly, she'd agreed to beyond pie.

9

IF EVER THERE WAS a moment of regret over food, Grace encountered it the second the last mouthful of the best chocolate cream pie in the world slid down her throat. She didn't want the experience to end. Yes, it was *pie*, but it was *amazing* pie. It was silky and sweet and smooth all wrapped up in the lightest pastry shell with the tallest peaked cream on top. And now it was gone.

Caught between the urge to lick her plate and groan from overindulgence, she glanced up at Justin. "Is it wrong to actually suffer remorse over the passing of a slice of pie?"

"Not when it's Mom's pie." Justin licked his fork before resting it on his empty plate. "She's a freaking pastry *master*."

"I want another piece but I'll die if one more bite of food passes through my lips." Setting her fork down, she slid low in the booth until her head rested against the bolster. "You couldn't have eaten like this every day. You'd be in a diabetic coma."

He huffed out a laugh and shook his head. "Nah. We didn't get dessert very often."

"Why?"

"Just the way it was." He tugged at his shirt collar, his

Adam's apple bobbing. "What about you? Your mom a good cook?"

The idea of her mother in the kitchen was so absurd she couldn't contain the bitter laugher that sliced through the momentary silence between them. "My mom doesn't cook."

Justin's brows shot up. "At all?"

"At all." She skimmed her hands down her sides, an electric jolt passing through her when his gaze followed her every move. "Body by Chef Boyardee, baby."

"Thank you, Chef," he said softly, gaze locked on her breasts.

Warmth bloomed in her, feminine and decidedly sexual—and entirely unwanted. She shifted in her seat, rubbing her thighs together while she wished madly for some pithy comeback, something that would be funny and right for the moment, something that would leave her with the last word.

He leaned forward and folded his arms on the table. "It's *so* wrong, what I'm thinking. Decidedly not professional."

That worked.

Justin reached out and took one of her hands, rolling it over and uncurling the fingers one by one until her palm lay face up and exposed. He gently traced a finger along her palm, first the long lines and then the short.

Her hand spasmed. "That tickles."

He peered at her through heavily lidded eyes. "I really want to—"

"Do you two care for refills?" Darcy asked, pausing at their table.

Justin let go of Grace's hand and casually leaned back. "We're good, Mom."

"Could a mother have shown up at a worse moment on a date?" Darcy set her coffee carafe down and wiped her hand across her brow. "I apologize."

"It's fine, Darcy. Truly. It's not a date." Grace settled her hands in her lap but couldn't stop herself from wringing them. The urge to explain nothing untoward had been happening hovered on the tip of her tongue, but it would be a lie.

Justin had been seducing her. Hell, if she were honest, he'd been seducing her from the moment he'd asked her to lunch. He just hadn't realized it. How could he? How could he possibly understand what it meant to her to be part of this microcosm of normality, where love and laughter and shared meals were common? How could he even pretend to grasp what it meant to her to experience his raw affection? Things that were so normal to him were nothing less than granted wishes to her, and it put the two of them immeasurably far apart on the scale of have and have-not. He was rich in ways she'd always been poor, and, despite the building sexual haze, it stung.

"It's probably best we head to the bus stop. Don't want to be late returning from lunch on day one." Grace aimed for cheerful but knew she achieved something much closer to a morbid grin.

"Don't go on my account," Darcy all but pleaded. "I'll give you two space. Just signal if you need anything."

"Really, it's fine. We have a meeting, and I want to prepare." She nodded at Justin and forced a smile. "I'll meet you at the office?"

Darcy absently straightened their table. "I'd like to make this up to you. Have dinner with us Wednesday evening."

Grace's chin rose so fast she nearly ended up with whiplash. "Really, you don't have to—"

"Nonsense," Darcy interjected. "While I appreciate that Justin brought you to the diner and let me feed you, it's not the same as welcoming you into our home and sharing a meal."

Her tone was so firm, so full of that mysterious parental power, Grace wasn't sure how to argue.

"That's a great idea." Justin met her gaze, his guileless blue eyes seeming to challenge her to defy his mother.

"What will you make?" From the wide-eyed glances, Grace's sudden question surprised everyone. Including herself.

Darcy composed herself first. "Well, I suppose that's up to you."

Justin glanced between the two of them. "How do you feel about chicken potpie?"

"Homemade?"

"Yes."

"I've never had it." The admission was somehow difficult.

Justin's chin whipped round, and he considered her with open curiosity. "You've never had chicken potpie?"

"Not homemade," she said mulishly, wondering what in the world had crawled under her skin. It was as if she was experiencing her own version of *Alien* right here in the diner. Or *The Exorcist.* "No."

Justin wordlessly considered her as Darcy commandeered the conversation. "That settles it. Justin can pick you up before dinner and—"

"Would you teach me to make it?" Grace's quiet question stopped the older woman dead in her conversational tracks.

Darcy gave a gentle smile. "Come about an hour and a half early? Say, five-thirty? The girls will be home by then so it might be a little tight in the kitchen, but I've always believed a crowded kitchen is a sign of a happy home. And actually Justin makes a better potpie. He can teach you."

JUSTIN COULDN'T HAVE planned that better if he'd tried, getting Darcy to corner Grace into coming to dinner. Granted, dinner with his family wouldn't be sexy, but it would be undeniably intimate. And it meant he'd gotten Grace to commit to spending more time with him outside the office. He'd teach her to cook and chat her up.

All forward mental momentum stalled at that particular curve. The expression on Grace's face when she'd asked Darcy to teach her, the way her voice had almost caught in her throat, it was yet more evidence of Grace's fragility. "Body by Chef Boyardee," she'd said, right after she'd laughed bitterly when he'd asked if her mother cooked. Clearly the woman was absent, but how? Why? He wanted to protect Grace from anyone who caused her pain, but right now that included him, so he'd have to tread carefully.

"Justin?"

He refocused on her. "Huh?"

A faint smile played around her lips. "If we don't go, we're going to be late."

"Right." Standing, he dumped some money on the table. "I'm out, people," he called.

A chorus of goodbyes rang out and he absently waved before catching the expression on Grace's face. He paused before glancing over his shoulder to see if something was amiss. Nothing. His brow creased. "What? What is it?"

She shook her head, her gaze locked on the floor.

"Clearly it's something. Fess up." Gesturing for her to go first, he followed her out of the restaurant. Watching her pert ass sway under that pencil skirt was certifiable torture.

He let her maintain her silence until they got to the bus stop. "You're going to have to communicate with me at some point, Grace. Might as well start now."

When she finally answered, she just stared down the street as if she was waiting for a glimpse of the bus. "I don't *have* to converse with you over anything but the practicum. The sooner you get that through your head, the happier this temporary work assignment will be for both of us."

Well, that smarted. "Right. There's a small problem with viewing things in such a limited way, though."

Still staring down the street, her answer was uninterested. "Which is?"

Uninterested just wouldn't do. He spun her around and pulled her into his arms in one fluid movement. His mouth found hers before she could voice her protest. He moved with clear intent and without consideration for who might be nearby. It was irrelevant. He wanted to show her what the moment meant to him. It was like some compulsion that drove him to mindlessly go where his heart led. Let the cards fall where they may.

She made an unintelligible sound even as she fisted his jacket and pulled him forward, closer.

Justin delved into her mouth, the urge to earn her capitulation urging him on like he was a thoroughbred in the final stretch of a high-stakes race. He didn't wait for her invitation. Instead, he simply took pleasure and sought to give twice as much in return.

Running his hands into her hair, he cupped her head, angled it for better access and took what was so crucial to him. Gave her what she wanted. A dark and demanding desire reared its head when Grace responded, pulling his body more firmly against hers.

Yes. This. More. With her, his mind purred. *Only her.*

Lips and teeth and tongue, he fought to own the moment, to own her. Her breath skated across his cheek on every exhale, scalding him, no doubt branding him. She tasted of chocolate cream pie, presented undiluted temptation, smelled like an invitation to sin.

He slid his hand around her waist and pulled at her shirt, untucking it just enough that he could slip his fingers under the waistband of her skirt. Skin to skin was his undoing. "Grace," he whispered into her mouth.

"Stop," she wheezed. "Stop it, Justin." Pushing at his

chest, she stumbled away a couple of steps and dragged a hand across her mouth. Her hair was a riot of loose curls. Her cheeks flushed a pretty pink that told a tale of passion nearly unleashed. Nearly.

Not close enough.

"You said lunch," she said on a heavy breath. *"Lunch."*

All his blood had flooded to his groin, and his brain wasn't working. "We had lunch."

"We're on the clock."

Reality blew through him like a bomb blast.

"You preach to me about doing the right thing, about how I'm not supposed to impugn your honor because it's somehow holy territory." Her chest heaved. The green of her eyes was wild. "Well, you just violated the code of ethics without blinking, and you did it right after you broke your word to *me*."

"You're right about us being on the clock. You're just as right about me not being fair." He stepped in closer. "But understand this, Grace Cooper. I want you. I've wanted you for years, and now that I've had a taste of you, settling for being near you isn't enough. Not even *remotely*. Lunch wasn't enough. Dinner won't *be* enough. I want more than you do, clearly, so my job is to change your mind. Don't expect me to lie around and wait for you to get on board with the idea because we're on a tight timeline. I'll push at and irritate you, no doubt. But in the end?" He curled a finger under her chin and lifted. "You make me lose my mind in the best possible way. I'm not willing to give that up over a little difference of opinion. You…this thing between us…it's all worth the fight, Grace. As for my ethics? I know what just happened between us, and it was, *is*, bigger than words on paper. Nothing that happens will change my opinion."

Her mouth opened and closed wordlessly. "We're technically working together, no matter how short an assignment this is. You can't act on every impulse you have."

He planted his fists on his hips and closed his eyes for a second, focusing on slowing his breathing and regaining control of the moment. "You're right. We're on the clock. If you want to report me for sexual harassment, I won't contest your claim."

"What?" she exclaimed. "No. I just want you to think. *Think*, Justin. And honor what you said you'd do."

"I never promised anything."

"You said lunch, as colleagues." The accusation was small, lacking the force of conviction he would have expected.

"And you're the one who said there was nothing between us."

"There isn't anything between us. When this internship is over, I'm moving to Baltimore. Permanently. I can't afford to get hung up wondering if this thing between us meant anything, Justin. The only way I can be happy is with a clean break, so this has to stop. *You* have to stop."

He made a show of smoothing his jacket down, fighting to keep his hands steady at her talk of leaving. "That's where you're wrong. I don't have to accept your word as final on the matter. See, unless I'm mistaken, that was a pretty damn passionate kiss. Should I assume you treat every guy to that particular pleasure?"

"You know I don't!" She shoved her hair off her face and gazed down the street with clear desperation. "Bus is almost here."

"This isn't finished, Grace."

She closed her eyes and took a deep breath that strained her breasts against the buttons of her shirt. "It's over, Justin. Whatever you believe is happening between us? You're wrong."

She angled her body to step into the bus before the doors were completely open.

He watched her move to the rear of the vehicle and take the only available seat. That was fine. He'd have given it to her, anyway. What he wouldn't give her was the satisfaction of hearing him say this was over. It wasn't. Not by a long shot.

He couldn't afford to lose his job and he wasn't going to cost her hers, but he'd never felt this way about any other woman. Two weeks from now she was moving to Baltimore. That meant he had a finite window of time to change her mind. He had to take the risks, ethics be damned. Granted, he did his best in life to take the high road when he could. But when the desired result couldn't be achieved by following a predetermined route, well, sometimes it meant taking risks and traveling more—even highly— questionable roads to get to where you most needed to be in the end. And in a weird way, the people at Second Chances would probably understand that better than most.

Stepping onto the bus, he took a spot near the driver. That didn't stop him from remembering her smooth skin beneath his fingers only moments before. Speaking of…

He twisted his hand around, confused by the long, shallow scratch that ran the length of his finger. The zipper on her skirt must have a bent tooth.

Ignoring the burning cut, he let himself sway with the bus as it moved, all the while considering his next move. It would have to be both cautious and bold. Never an easy combination.

He grinned. That only meant whatever he came up with would be memorable, hopefully in all the right ways. It would have to spell things out very clearly.

He wasn't about to give up on her.

10

GRACE'S HANDS SHOOK. She couldn't get them to stop as she put together the client file for their one-thirty meeting. The second time she dropped the two-prong clasp, she shut the folder and dropped her hands to her lap. This...this...*thing* with Justin had to stop. He couldn't keep rattling her, taking her to lunch at an emotional haven and then kissing her senseless at the bus stop. The *bus stop*, for heaven's sake.

Her fingers absently stroked her parted lips as she remembered the way he'd taken over, taken responsibility from her and allowed her to simply experience the kiss. He'd tasted like bacon. The faintest facial hair had begun to grow in on his jaw, brushing her soft skin and making her that much more aware of him. His hands had woven through her hair, claiming control of even the way she tilted her head. Her heart had crashed against her ribs, and heavy pulses had landed between her thighs with undisguised physical craving. She'd wanted him.

She still wanted him.

He'd left her unfulfilled. The unapologetic bulge in his pants said he hadn't been unaffected, either. Had they been somewhere more private, she probably would have pulled a King Kong and scaled him like the Empire State Building. Thank God they *had* been in public. She couldn't let this get any further out of hand. She couldn't get more involved and maintain her sanity. She couldn't let him derail all she'd worked for over the years by feeding the fierce attraction between them.

"Get it under control, Cooper," she whispered, reaching for the folder.

"Who're you talking to?"

She jerked so hard she sent the container of two-prong clasps flying. They scattered across the floor, some sliding under the desk while others gently wedged themselves under Justin's shoes.

"Office-supply rebellion?" One corner of his mouth curled up in a lopsided smile as he closed the door. "That doesn't strike me as your speed, Grace. If you were going to throw something at me, I would have expected something more in line with, oh, the chair."

"Duly noted. 'Boss expects physical abuse and property destruction.'"

He snorted and shook his head, bending over to pick up the file clasps. "I went over the notes for our one-thirty. The patient's got some serious anger issues. He's being courted by one of Seattle's most violent gangs and already has an impressive arrest record. Assault, destruction of public property, possession of a stolen firearm and possession with the intent to distribute. The last is what landed him here."

Grace grabbed a pad of paper and began taking notes. "Which gang?"

"Deuce-8."

She stopped abruptly. Eyes wide, she fought the urge to shiver. "Whoa."

"Yeah." Justin deposited the clasps near Grace. Taking a deep breath, he rolled his head left and right, popping his neck, before dropping into his chair. "Nothing better than baptism by fire."

"I'm not Baptist."

He grinned. "Neither am I."

"Welcome to the fold."

His laughter was deep and heartfelt. "You kill me."

"Second note to self. 'Boss instructed me to kill him.'"

"Ha." Sliding down in his chair, he crossed his hands over his abs. "I set up the therapy room. Can you do me a favor?"

She hesitated before answering. "Sure."

"Nothing nefarious."

"Okay."

"I want you to take some very particular notes." He leaned forward, arms resting on his knees. "While I'm talking to him, I want you to surreptitiously sketch whatever tattoos he's advertising. I'm going to bet he's got quite a few and that none of them spell out *Mom*."

"Right. They'll have meaning," she murmured, scribbling. "We might have to consult a member of the police's gang unit to figure out what they mean. He's not going to own it. At least, not right away. And somehow I doubt there's much available to the average person in the way of a field guide for amateur tattoo identifications. Can't imagine there's a huge call for that kind of stuff at local bookstores."

Justin reached out and gently touched her knee.

Heat crept up her legs. A whimper caught at the base of her throat. Her eyes snapped from his fingers to his face.

"You're pretty calm about this. That's damned attractive."

"It's my job to remain calm and objective." If his voice was deep and sexually charged, hers was full-on Marilyn Monroe breathy.

Justin's eyes blazed, blue irises deepening as his pupils widened. He scooted to the edge of his seat and wheeled over to Grace. Propping his hands on the arms of her very stationary chair, he leaned into her personal space. "Do I make you nervous?"

"You make me crazy." The admission snuck out without her conscious permission.

"I can settle for crazy."

"You can't just kiss me whenever you want, Justin."

He arched a brow. "What if you kiss me?"

"Not going to happen."

"And why is that?"

"Lunch was a mistake. I try to learn from those. I won't be kissing you again."

Surprise flashed across his face. "That was a mistake?"

"Yeah." Her answer was so faint she followed it up with a vigorous nod to make sure he got the point.

"I don't agree."

"Please don't do this, Justin."

"Do what?"

"Don't make saying no to you any harder on me than it already is."

The phone beeped and the receptionist's voice filled the air. "Gavin Stills is here, Dr. Maxwell. He's waiting in the lobby."

"Saved by the intercom," he murmured.

"I'm sorry?" the receptionist asked.

"Nothing. Thank you, Mallory."

The woman's voice dropped an octave or three. "Of course." The phone clicked as she disconnected.

Grace forced a smile. "Seems you've got a new admirer."

"The only admirer I want is you."

"You charmer, you." She blew out a deep breath and fought to keep from telling him just how much she wanted to say yes to him, to agree to give this a shot. Instead what she said was, "Get it together, Dr. Maxwell. Your first official patient is waiting."

It was the best she could do to close a conversation that was rattling her, particularly considering the fact he seemed pretty collected. She was the one who was falling apart.

JUSTIN'S HEAD WASN'T QUITE in the game as he left the office, Grace at his side. Part of him was focused on the fact he was seeing his first patient. An equal, maybe even larger, part couldn't shift its focus from the woman at his side. He wanted to finish this particular conversation with Grace. Leaving it like they had seemed as though it would undermine the very things he wanted from her, things that were very personal, undeniably real and unapologetically involved. She'd shut him down before he'd been able to voice what he needed her to hear. That wasn't acceptable. He needed to set this straight or he'd never be able to focus on the kid who needed his full attention.

Slowing, Justin gently took Grace's arm and pulled her to a stop, stepping in front of her. "Our conversation isn't over. We both know we have to focus on the job right now, but that doesn't buy you an out from hearing what I have to say. I'm going to leave you with this." He moved in closer, forcing her to lift her chin to meet his stare. "This thing between us? It's not wrong, Grace. That it's hard to keep shutting me down should tell you something."

She squared her shoulders. "I never said it was wrong. I said, in summary, it's not a possibility I'm willing to explore. My life begins when I get out of Seattle, Justin, and your life is here. That puts us at an impasse."

A sense of despondency scored his heart. She couldn't simply leave him under the false pretense that this was how it had to be. He couldn't live with the idea she would dismiss their night together as if it hadn't happened. It *had* happened, would happen again—and again—if he got his way. But if she wanted to play stubborn, he could play. It just meant a change of tactics.

Resting his hands on her shoulders, he met her stare. "Okay, no more bus-stop moments. If you want me, you initiate the contact. I'm stepping away."

She opened her mouth to respond but the overhead PA-system chime interrupted her. "Dr. Maxwell to the lobby. Dr. Maxwell to the lobby, please."

"Our client's waiting." He swept an arm out to invite her to proceed down the hall.

She moved past him wordlessly, chancing a single look over her shoulder as she moved along at a sharp clip.

Justin caught up to her so they rounded the corner to the front lobby as a team.

The teen waiting on them sat in the hard plastic chair and emitted an air of arrogant disregard Justin recognized. Wearing a black, flat-billed ball cap and a denim jacket marked with Deuce-8's colors, the kid looked caught between bored and belligerent. Low-slung, superbaggy hip-hop jeans bunched around his ankles, the pockets covered in embroidered graffiti. His white tank top was pristine, as were his white Air Jordan shoes. In all, Justin rang up a mental $800 in threads. No one from this kid's neighborhood had that much money for clothes unless they were supplementing their income, heavily, and Justin wasn't thinking a second job working nights stocking shelves. No, this kind of supplement cost people their lives.

Hands loose at his sides, Justin walked up and loomed over the teen just a bit. "Hey. You must be Gavin Stills."

The kid stood, his junior pecs hitting Justin's ribs. "Back off me, man."

"I don't think so."

"You wanna throw down? Cuz I'll bleed you out right here, right now." Posturing, the teen bumped into Justin.

Justin was well aware of how gang infrastructure

worked. Only the brutal truth and showing a stronger hand than the kid's own would garner his respect. Justin had been in the exact same place, faced down a counselor in the same way in this very lobby. "Yeah? And here I'd been told you were smart."

"You just call me stupid?" the teen snapped, shoving the bill of his hat around so he had an unimpeded view of Justin.

"You heard me, but let me make it simpler. I'm all that stands between you and juvie, and you're right there on the edge of being old enough to do real time. That would make you the prison's baby boy, and I don't think you'd like that too much. So it's up to you. We can figure out who's tougher right here, right now, or we can talk. Personally? I'd rather talk, but it's your choice."

Gavin gazed up through narrow eyes, adjusting his pants repeatedly. Justin recognized the move as a threatening gesture and wondered, briefly, if he was going to have to pin the kid to the ground while they called the cops. Not the best first impression to make, but he had to earn the kid's buy-in to the program, and superior strength was the only thing he'd respect.

"First rule?" Justin said so softly the kid was forced to stop rustling his pants to hear him. "No one comes in here and threatens me."

"You said first. What are the others?"

"Appears you *are* a smart kid. There are two others. Second rule is that you don't wear gang colors when you come in here. Period." When Gavin started to argue, Justin crossed his substantial arms across his chest and forced the kid back a step. "No. Gang. Colors."

"A'ight, a'ight."

"Third and final rule? No violence on these grounds. You break that rule, I call the cops and your freedom is revoked by a judge. No warnings, no plea bargains, and I won't be speaking up on your behalf in court. Got it?"

"I can hear just fine."

"Then I'm going to assume you accept the rules."

"Whatever."

"You have a chance here, Gavin. Don't screw it up."

"I get it. Are we done?" he asked, but beneath the belligerence, Justin heard uncertainty.

Excellent. It meant he'd thrown the kid off his game. Score one for the counselor.

"C'mon." Justin moved away. "Let me introduce you to my assistant. Grace?" He watched as she closed the distance between them, her movements both confident and calm. "Gavin, this is Grace Cooper. She's finishing her degree in psychology, so she'll be sitting in with us for the next two weeks."

"You got your own Vanna White?" His eyes moved over Grace. "That's cool."

"Actually, I prefer Black Widow. She's hot, a little mouthy, smart as hell and she totally kicks ass."

Justin looked at her askance, trying to gauge what she was up to.

"You a comic fan?" Gavin asked.

"Marvel fan, yes. C'mon. They've got great heroes."

Gavin caught himself midlaugh and shrugged. "Black Widow your favorite?"

"I'm definitely more fond of Thor."

"Such a chick thing to say."

"Hey, the guy can take a beating and still get up. That's hot."

Gavin eyed her with new interest. "So you like that he's tough?"

"Well, yeah."

"What else?"

"You'll have to talk to me to find out. I don't dish comics with folks who can't hang with the conversation."

He grinned. "I can hang."

"Let's go, then."

Justin gaped, watching as they started down the hall, the two of them chatting away about comics. Shaking himself out of it, he took off after them, fighting not to hurry but, instead, to keep his gait slow and sure.

He entered the therapy room several seconds after the duo did. They were settling in, still chatting about inane stuff. Grace had her notepad out but hadn't made any notes despite the fact the kid had shed his jacket and his ink was prominently displayed.

Pulling up his chair, Justin waited for a brief lull before inserting himself into the conversation. "So, Gavin, what's going on?"

The kid glanced between him and Grace, clearly unsure who was the more comfortable to talk to. His attention stalled on Grace.

Justin smiled inwardly, proud that Grace had been able to establish a connection with the kid so quickly.

Finally, the teen focused on a spot on the floor somewhere in between them. "My parole officer said I had to come talk to the shrink here."

Justin considered him. "You seem a little young to already have your own parole officer."

"Old enough," Gavin bit out.

"Sure." Justin waited for the silence to stretch enough that the kid glanced up. "So, this was part of your plea deal?"

Twisting the bill of his hat to the front, the teen slouched in his chair. "Something like that, yeah."

Justin picked up a pen and began to roll it between his fingers. "Talk to me about what you've got going on that might land you in front of the judge."

Gavin sighed. "It ain't nothin'. Cops just get worked up over stupid stuff."

"Probably, but the longer you sit here avoiding my questions, the longer we're going to drag this session out."

Dark, angry eyes glanced his way before the youth refocused on the floor. "Fine."

"I'll put this out there again. Talk to me about what's going on that landed you on the cops' radars."

Gavin lifted his chin, the look on his face unreadable. "I got this gig making some extra cash on the side."

Grace immediately interjected. "Hold up, hold up. You can front all you want with other people, but in here? You come clean. It's honesty or nothing."

Justin's eye twitched. If the kid chose nothing, the conversation was over.

Gavin stared up at Grace, jaw set. He considered her for a moment then gave a finite nod. "Fine. I got a job as a courier for a guy."

"I take it you weren't delivering letters unless they were *H* or *X*," Grace drawled.

Gavin snorted. "Pretty much."

"Decent money?"

The kid grinned. "Better than 'decent.' I mean, I bought these threads with my own Benjamins."

"You understand that green came at a cost, though."

"So?" His shoulders hunched. "I didn't hurt nobody."

The conversation went on as Justin watched with a combination of amazement and amusement. He'd seriously underestimated Grace and her ability to handle this kid. Then she said something that made the skin on the back of his neck prickle.

"Are you sure you didn't cause anyone harm by serving as a courier?"

Gavin's response was quick. "No. I didn't put drugs in nobody's hands."

Justin interceded. "Sure, but you took the drugs from the main man to his distributor. That *did* put drugs in someone's hands."

"Man, I didn't sell drugs to nobody."

"Your rap sheet said you were charged with intent to distribute."

"I was framed."

"You've admitted you were couriering, Gavin. Don't go south on me now." Justin slouched in his chair, the picture of a relaxed guy in a common conversation. "It's important that you realize the choices you make have repercussions. You chose to act as courier. Your choice put the drugs in the hands of someone who sold it to someone else. You follow?"

"You're talking simple economics, supply and demand."

Justin had been where this kid was, understood what it meant that he'd learned so much about the economics of drug commerce. Gavin was in deeper than they'd realized. *So damn young.* This kid was a mirror image of who he'd been and where he'd been headed. His heart ached for Gavin, and he fought the instinct to do whatever he had to in order to save the teen from a life that was no life at all. *Psychology 101. You can't save them all.*

"What?" Gavin asked childishly for all he was clearly higher up in Deuce-8's ranks than Justin had been led to believe.

"Nothing. Just thinking. Tell me something, Gavin. What's your mom like?"

"You leave my mom out of this," he yelled, surging to his feet. "You don't got no right to bring her into this room!"

Justin put his hands up, palms out, in a "backing off" gesture. "It's cool. I'll leave it alone."

"Gavin, stop." Grace's calm command cut through the explosive tension. "You might live in a world where violence is accepted, even encouraged, but I won't allow you to subject me to that. Do you understand?"

The teen resettled himself in his chair. "Sorry, Ms. Grace."

"Forgiven. Now, tell *me* something. What's the one thing that you want me to know about you?"

Justin watched Grace manage the kid and realized she'd made the right move in taking over the conversation. It made sense Gavin would talk to Grace and reject Justin, given a choice between the sexes. Clearly, his mother meant something to him. Justin doubted the kid's father was in the picture. The only male with any authority he respected would be those higher up in Deuce. So Justin would try harder, work harder.

The timer went off and he stood, casting Grace an assessing glance. Eyes bright and cheeks slightly flushed, he saw she was invigorated by how well the session had gone. He was proud of her. Gavin had gravitated to her like a moon caught up in a planet's gravitational pull. Justin understood the draw. There was something about her that made you want to be closer to her, physically and emotionally. It had started so long ago for him he'd almost forgotten what that first hit of Grace could do to a guy. Gavin might be a kid, but he was on the cusp of adulthood. He was no more immune to Grace than Justin was.

He shoved his hands in his pockets and Gavin tensed. Slowly, he removed them. "Nothing in there but some loose change and lint. Okay?" The teen nodded and Justin let out the breath he'd inadvertently been holding. "Let's leave it here and pick things up again Wednesday. You're in three days a week for how many weeks?"

"Four."

"I'll note that in your chart. It'll give us a chance to get to know each other." He offered the young man a hand, held it out there and waited while it was considered. Slowly, as if Justin posed an undefined threat, Gavin reached out and gave him a quick, firm shake. "Cool. Catch up with you Wednesday, then."

He was out the door with only a brief glance at Grace.

"Kid's got a crush on you." Justin gathered up his notes and turned to find Grace writing like mad. "What's up?"

She didn't look away from her notepad as she answered. "Give me five—ten—minutes. I have to get this stuff down."

He shrugged and started for the door. "I'll be in my office when you're done."

"Justin?"

"Yeah?"

"Thanks."

That stopped him. "For what?"

"Letting me run the session."

"You were great in there. Besides, it wasn't so much about me letting you, Grace. The kid cleaved to you. If you have a better chance to reach him, you should lead the session."

She nodded. "Right. I just…"

"What?"

"I won't be here for the entire four weeks he's scheduled. Is it smart to let him get invested in me as a counselor?"

He leaned against the door frame and considered her, his mind working frantically but with absolute clarity. "I'd rather let it play out and see where it's going to go in the time we have. If we work together, we might be able to stop his behavior from escalating." Pausing, he considered how much to say, how much to offer her, and settled with "I want him out of that lifestyle, Grace."

"You want to save the world," she mused.

"I'm not sure about the world, but a kid… I want Gavin out of Deuce-8."

"It's personal, isn't it."

Her statement was so matter-of-fact, so nonquestioning and nonjudgmental, that he found himself fighting not to let the truth pour out, to open up to her about his descent into darkness. The words were there, parked on the tip of his tongue, held in check only by pride and fear. He'd overcome his past, but it would always be there. Tattoo coverup jobs were great, but beneath his ink lay a tattoo identical to the one Gavin sported—the deuce with two dots parallel to the point and a sideways figure eight between them.

No, now wasn't the time to confess past transgressions to Grace. That time might never come. All the more reason to keep his mouth shut now when emotions were running high.

"Justin?"

His chin snapped up. "Let's wrap this one up. We've got another appointment in thirty minutes. Sixteen-year-old girl with suicidal ideation."

The glow in Grace's face faded. "I'll be ready."

Without another word, he left the room. She was too much of a temptation in so many ways. And her quick statement that she wouldn't be here for Gavin's full four-week counseling assignment... It had stolen his breath, made his mind go blank. He rubbed clammy palms over his thighs. He had to make her see that staying, taking the risk, was worth it.

That *he* was worth it.

11

GRACE DREW THE tattoos she'd been able to see with as much detail as she could remember, but her mind was wandering. Why had Justin let her, as a brand-new graduate, take the lead in the therapy room? Sure, he was also a new grad, but he had his doctorate. She only had her master's. Not bad, but definitely not comparable to a PhD. Big difference in practical theory and clinical exposure. He'd seen patients on campus and had assisted in running trials for the psychology department. Still, this was different. This was his first real job.

Her hand stilled mid-design. This *wasn't* Justin's first real job, though. He'd worked as a stripper and as a teaching assistant for the university for years. He'd worked far longer than she'd given him credit for, at least initially. She'd dismissed his work history as inconsequential, and that was incredibly unfair. She had been so busy holding him at arm's length personally that she had dismissed him professionally. He deserved better than that, deserved credit for his efforts and experience. That knowledge didn't make it any easier to accept his praise, though.

And what about the personal aspect? Hadn't she dismissed him just as effectively in her private life? That he might actually care about her on some genuine level terrified her. So, yeah. She might have dismissed him out of hand.

Her mind flashed on the kiss at the bus stop. The kiss had been spectacular, full of the same passion Justin had shown the night they'd been at the hotel. But the significance was far more complex. When they'd first been together, they'd set the rules. One night. No holding back. No apologies and no regrets. She'd adhered to those rules to the letter, as they'd suited her. There was no room in her plans for sentiment, no matter that she might crave more than she'd bargained for.

Liar.

There was no "might" to it.

Flinching, she flipped to a new page and began to doodle, not thinking about what she was doing. Justin's face emerged. It was a good rendition, illustrating his dark hair, lush mouth and piercing eyes. The planes of his cheeks were a bit hollow in her rendition, so she shaded this way and that before she had the picture right to her mind's eye.

Beneath his image she wrote and underlined a single word. *Impossible.* Nothing described what was going on between them any better than that. She couldn't give up the education she'd fought to obtain, and she wouldn't risk staying in proximity to her mother on a maybe. If she'd learned anything from that woman, it was that relationships couldn't be counted on to solve a person's unhappiness. That was up to her to do. She had to seize life by the throat and wrestle it to the ground until opportunity was hers to seize. She'd settle for nothing else, particularly on a maybe from someone who had wounded her emotionally. It would be sheer foolishness.

Ripping the sheet of paper free, she wadded it up and tossed it into the garbage can. No quick pen sketch would ever do the man justice, any more than a single word could describe how she felt about him. She grabbed her stuff and left the therapy room.

Justin was in his office, dark head bent low over some form or another. He glanced up. "Hey. How'd the sketches go?"

"Good. At least I think they're good." She handed the pages over, uncertain she'd caught what he wanted.

Justin's gaze ran over the four pages of drawings she'd done. "Holy crow, Grace. These are amazing. You didn't mention you were an artist."

"I'm not," she said softly. "I just like to draw." *And paint. Oh, she loved to paint.*

Finger tracing the Deuce-8 symbol, he shook his head. "Seriously. You're incredible."

She'd wanted to hear those words from him, but now they were tinged with irony. She'd wanted someone to tell her she was special, but now that someone had, she was going to walk away from him in two weeks.

She regretted for the hundredth time agreeing to dinner at Justin's house. Inundated with Justin and his family, she knew instinctually exactly what would happen. She'd make dinner, Darcy would praise her profusely because that's who she was, and Grace would soak up her praise like a desiccated sponge dropped in a sink full of water. Justin would help her cook, directing her with light touches, complimenting her not only with words but with his eyes, his body. She'd feed him. The intimacy of that gesture, for her, would be her undoing. No, she had to cancel. It sucked. Man, it sucked. But it was better for everyone.

"Do you want help with your case notes?" Justin set the pad aside, his eyes locked on her.

"I—I'm sure I can manage," she stuttered, her determination to cancel dinner slipping away as she watched him.

He smiled. "Let's get cracking then."

"Aren't you done with your notes already?" He should have been.

"I waited on you so we could do them together." Her brow furrowed and he chuckled. "You're worried I didn't do my job."

"No." *Yes.*

"It's fine, Grace. I dictated what I needed to and I'll work from that to fill in any blanks."

"Oh," she said stupidly. "I didn't consider dictation."

His gaze narrowed and a wicked smile curled the corners of his lips. "It's quite a useful…tool."

The sexual innuendo rolled over her like a heat wave. She was suddenly sweating and needed air. "You want me to go to Starbucks and get us drinks?" Spending the extra money was foolish, but if it got her out of the office and away from him? It was totally worth it.

"There's coffee in the break room. I'd rather you stay right here and work with me. Side by side."

Damn. She'd hoped she could bribe him. Settling her chair in front of the desk, she couldn't help but draw in the clean, crisp smell that defined Justin.

He slid in closer so their elbows touched. "Let's get this party started."

His low, smooth voice churned up things that were better left dormant in her, cravings for more from him than just the one night they'd had. He was offering more, but how far could things possibly go in the two weeks she was here? And when she was finished? How could she leave a man like this behind? Then again, how could she not? Could she risk everything she'd worked for on the slight chance that this thing between them might go somewhere?

"No," she said aloud, startling both of them.

"No party?" he asked lightly.

"Sorry. I was answering a personal thought and it slipped out."

He leaned back in his chair and draped his arm around her. "What thought?"

"I don't want to discuss it."

"Was it work related?"

"No," she answered too quickly, giving him insight into her that she didn't necessarily want him to have.

"Was it about me?" The quiet question held an undertone of hope.

"Yes." Her answer, just as quiet, hurt. "But I don't want to talk about it."

"Fair enough." He sat up, reached for his laptop and dragged it over. "Let's get started."

"That's it? 'Fair enough'?"

"You said you didn't want to talk about it. I respect that."

Grace was so confused. She wanted him to press, wanted him to be more determined to know what she was thinking just as much as she wanted him to leave this, and her, alone. Frowning, she reached for her pad of paper. "I need a laptop."

"I'll see what I can do about that," he answered, sliding his laptop in front of her. "Use mine for now."

"What will you use?"

"My personal computer." When she hesitated, he pressed. "It's fine, Grace. I brought it with me." He retrieved an older machine and set it in front of his workspace. "You can argue with me about it later. Right now, we've got to get the notes in before our next client."

She settled in to work, forcing her mind to replay the session as she tried desperately to ignore the brush of his arm against hers, the heat from his body and the sound of his breathing.

The knowledge she was going to have to edit the hell out of her case notes struck her as funny, and she smiled.

No way was she going to manage to get this right with him so close.

It just wasn't happening.

Yes! Justin wanted to shout to the heavens. She was thinking about him and it bothered her. That indicated she had thoughts she didn't want to have. He'd take it because it meant he'd succeeded in getting her to consider him, and likely them, on her own. Yeah, he'd take it.

Her body was so close he wanted to touch her, to trace the soft contours of her face, trail his fingers down her neck and across the modest expanse of décolletage she was displaying. He wanted to tease that slim glimpse of skin with his fingertips, make her nipples pucker under that proper shirt and hear her gasp with surprise. She always did, as though she was shocked at her response to him. He freaking loved that about her.

His stomach lurched at the word. *Love.* He could easily love her. He'd spent years watching her, wanting her, listening to her talk, hearing her defend her hypotheses to fellow students, seeing her kindness with those who didn't understand a concept, having her come by his office to talk. He'd known one night with her wouldn't be enough; he'd been half in love with her even before they'd made love. Experiencing her body, loving her physically? It had changed things between them, even if she didn't realize it yet. She would. He'd make sure of it.

"Justin? Which ICD-9 code would I use to classify 'save this kid's life'? Because I'm just not finding one."

Jolted back to the moment at hand, he glanced at her and grinned. "There's no superhero code in the medical indices. We'll have to come up with something creative, because I've heard that billing the state for these types of services can get dicey."

"Fair enough. I'll leave that part blank for now."

"We'll figure it out together." And they would, because she'd be here tomorrow and the next day. His heart rate doubled, the rush of blood making him light-headed. He pressed a hand to his forehead.

"Did I hurt your brain with the brilliant question?"

"Yes, you hurt my brain."

"Sorry." The smile in her voice was evident even if she wasn't showing one. His office phone rang, startling him. "Excuse me while I answer the Bat Cave line." He grabbed the phone. "Dr. Maxwell."

"Hey, Doc. I have this rash I can't seem to get rid of. It's on my—"

"Stop right there, sir. I know exactly what you're suffering from. Only immediate surgical intervention stands a chance of saving your life. I suggest a complete lobotomy, stat. Go to the nearest emergency room and advise them you're there on the advice of your psychologist."

His best friend, Eric, laughed. "Very funny, man. How's your first day going?"

"Awesome, actually. I've dealt with an overworked HR department, a director on a mission to run this place efficiently if it kills us all, a college intern I just happened to teach who is also hot as hell and a patient who loved the intern and shunned me."

Grace shoved his shoulder. "Shut up," she hissed.

"Well, if she's hot, I'd shun you, too. Grace Cooper?"

"How could you *possibly* know that?"

"Cass and I went by the diner for a late lunch. Darcy mentioned that we'd just missed you and your lovely *girlfriend* by a few minutes."

"She's not… That is, I don't mean to say… Damn it."

Eric laughed. "Don't worry. I totally get it. What are you guys doing for dinner tonight?"

"It's not like that, man." Justin pulled at his collar. Why couldn't he breathe?

"Come out with us. We're going to this dive bar Cass loves. They make mean nachos."

"You had me at *nachos*, but it'll probably just be…" His plan to make her see the potential between them by taking her to the diner hadn't exactly panned out. Maybe asking her out, introducing her to his friends, showing her he wasn't the ass she believed him to be, was a good idea. "I'm in recovery mode at the moment."

"With her?"

Thank God Eric understood. "Yeah."

"Stick your size twelve and a half in your mouth?"

"To the knee, my friend."

"Ouch. Been there, done that. Don't worry, I'll warn Cass and we'll be on our best behavior. You, though? You're on your own. I can only do so much to make you look good."

Justin laughed. "Understood. I'll see you there. Wait. Where? I have no idea where we're going."

"For such a bright guy, you're a bit of a dumbass at times."

"Address, please, before I release my minion on you. She's smart. So smart, in fact, I would imagine she could have you locked up tight in a padded cell before you figured out the straight jacket wasn't Cass's new kink."

Eric snickered. "Funny guy. We'll be down at Pandora's on Post Avenue."

"Deal. I'll look the address up online and be there… when?"

"We're going for dinner, so about sevenish. I would imagine we'll be there three or four hours."

"Cool. See you then."

"Bring her, Justin."

"Do my best."

"Later."

He hung up the phone, his hand lingering on the receiver.

Grace swiveled toward him. "Unless you've got a secret stash, I assume I'm the referenced minion?"

"My one and only."

The words hung in the air until she cleared her throat and twisted back to her computer screen. "I assume everything's okay?"

"Fine." His absent tone registered even with him and he forced a small smile. "Just have to figure out how to accomplish a particular goal."

"Which is?"

"Nothing. Forget it." He couldn't admit that winning her over was his mission for the evening. Before any winning could occur, he had to get her to agree to go.

"Okay." She resumed entering her notes, but her progress was notably slower.

An idea struck. Picking up the phone, he called his other close friend Levi.

"Hello?" he muttered.

"It's almost three o'clock, Sleeping Beauty."

"Nice try. You'll never be Prince Charming."

That hit a little close to home. "I could be if I tried."

"For what it's worth, I'm into the princesses. What do you want?"

"Get some coffee already."

"Means getting out of bed. It's too early for that kind of commitment to the day," Levi said around a yawn.

"Eric and Cass are going to Pandora's tonight. We're getting a few people together. Want to go?"

"Yeah. Sounds like fun." Bedclothes rustled and a feminine voice protested. Levi ignored her to ask, "What time?"

"About seven, seven-thirty."

"I'll be there. An opportunity to go out without the assless chaps is always welcome."

Justin laughed. "Ain't that the truth. No firemen, lumberjacks, sailors or construction workers allowed."

"Then I'm definitely in. See ya."

They hung up. Justin went back to his chart and forced himself to fill in some of the information before tilting his head toward Grace. "A few of my friends are getting together tonight. Want to come along? We're meeting at some dive bar that allegedly serves the best nachos in Seattle."

She hesitated long enough that Justin had to fight to not push, cajole or plead with her to say yes. Finally, *finally*, she looked over at him. "No construction workers, huh?"

"Nope. No cowboys, either."

"Shame. I'm rather fond of cowboys." She chewed her bottom lip for a moment. "Why are you inviting me?"

"I want to hang out with you. It's a group setting, public venue. Nothing nefarious. Just come out for a while. Enjoy yourself. You'll like the people who are going."

"It's not another 'lunch' situation?"

"I gave you my word—I won't push."

She ran a hand around the nape of her neck and shrugged one shoulder. "Sure. I'll come. When should I meet you there?"

"About seven-thirty. That'll give everyone time to be late and you won't end up waiting on us."

She laughed. "Your friends are always late?"

"Eric and Cass are awesome, but they're a new couple so...yeah, they tend to run late." Heat crept across his cheeks, and he grinned at his own awkwardness over his friends' sex lives. "Levi will be there, but he's rarely the first to arrive. Has this thing about being alone." And that might have been too much personal information on the guy, but it would explain him well enough she understood.

"And you?"

"If you're there at seven-thirty?" He leaned toward her, one corner of his mouth lifting in an approximation of a smile, thrilling at the way her lips parted and her breath caught. "I'll be there at seven to make sure you have a place at the table."

"Seven-thirty it is." She lowered her lids halfway and swayed toward him.

His heart stuttered and his palms grew slick.

"Now stop with the seductive crap and get back to work."

His laughter echoed through the near-empty room. "You're a total vixen."

"Nicest thing you've said to me all day."

"Then I haven't been nice enough."

She didn't comment but returned to her notes, leaving him to wonder what would happen if they kissed again.

His mind jumped to the image of her naked beneath him, writhing and calling his name. His cock swelled and he sought to regain his control before he was forced to stand up and let his burgeoning erection announce that his mind had been in the gutter.

No, not gutter. Not where Grace was concerned.

Seduction was the key phrase he had to focus on tonight. He would find the best way to show her who he was outside the club, outside the office. He'd come this far through hard work, determination and, more than once, self-sacrifice. He wanted her to see that. If he could, he might have a chance. His life was finally falling into place. But for the story to be worth telling, he had to get the girl.

No pressure.

12

GRACE STEPPED OFF the 68 bus and, head down, started the short walk home. Her address's only redeeming quality was that it put her close to the bus stop.

Fat raindrops began to fall. The clean scent dissipated the overwhelming smell of pot as she passed the first drug dealer's house.

No one had to tell her not to slow down, not to look left or right, not to notice too much. She'd grown up here, knew the streets and the dangers that lay in plain sight, as well as those that didn't.

There was no way she was going to stay in Seattle. Living anywhere near this hellhole she'd grown up in was out of the question. She wanted out, wanted to be thousands of miles away, to start a new life with none of the ugliness and poverty and fear that had been her life up until now. She wanted to cut ties with her mother and find a place to settle down, create roots and a sense of belonging, both to community and to someone special.

Justin's face flashed through her mind.

He'd shared his family with her, showed her what it was like to have roots, people who cared about him. And he'd opened the door to her, offering to let her be one of them for the last couple of weeks she'd be here.

But she couldn't get invested in these people and then

just leave. What he offered would only fuel her desire for him, because she found the way he treated his friends and extended family incredibly attractive. Okay, a little sexy, even.

She was so lost in thought she didn't notice the large man walking down the sidewalk until she'd almost run into him. Quickly stepping aside, she murmured, "Sorry."

"No problem, beautiful. Feel like making a man's evening and having a little fun in the process?"

"That's my daughter, Mitch." Her mother's venomous voice sliced through the air like a snake strike.

"Easy, Cindy. Just having a chat with the young lady. Didn't realize she was yours." He leaned close. "What a shame." Then he walked off.

The exchange made her skin crawl. It also reaffirmed her belief that her only hope for the life she wanted to make for herself laid far east of the state line.

Cindy stepped inside, letting the screen door slam shut so hard the glass panel rattled dangerously. Grace knew then she'd have to get in and out of the house as fast as possible if she wanted to avoid a confrontation.

She paused on the stoop, the smell of fresh cigarettes and whiskey wafting from the house. *Damn it.* Her mom was on the hard stuff again. That meant she was probably dabbling with drugs, too. How the woman passed the random drug screening at the factory was beyond Grace's comprehension.

Shoring up her emotional strength and pulling indifference around her like a protective cloak, she stepped inside the house.

Two weeks and counting. She could do anything for two weeks knowing freedom lay on the other side of this, her personal perdition.

Cindy sat sprawled on the couch in a dirty T-shirt and a pair of men's boxers. Her nails, thick and yellowed from smoking, were short and uneven. Dark roots showed where her long hair was parted, affirming blond wasn't her natural color. As if the burned ends didn't say it all.

"Stop staring." She took a long draw on her cigarette, eyeing Grace carefully. "Where'd you get the money for those new clothes?"

"I had some money left over from my last work-study job." Grace started through the living room, stepping around scattered pizza boxes, beer bottles and—ew—a condom wrapper. She couldn't help it. She glanced over and arched a brow. "Safe sex, huh? Your idea or his?"

"Mitch is a total wuss. Said he had to have the condom or no sex, so condom it was." Cindy's eyes narrowed and her mouth thinned into a mean, harsh line. "Right here on the sofa, Grace. Does that offend you, your highness? Huh, Miss Prim-and-Proper?"

She didn't slow down as she answered. "You can do whatever you want with your body wherever you want to do it."

Cindy stubbed out her cigarette. "Don't judge me, you little bitch. You ain't worth nothing. Never been good for anything but ruining my life."

Numb. Have to stay numb. "I'm not saying a word."

"You think you're so much better than us common folk since you went and got an education. But that piece of paper don't change the fact you *came* from common, you *are* common and you'll always *be* common."

Grace continued on to her bedroom without responding, opening her door and slipping inside.

Something glass hit the door behind her and shattered, the strong smell of liquor wafting up from the floor.

That's when the shakes started.

Maybe she wasn't as numb as she'd thought, or hoped, she was. It had been a long time since her mother had been conscious enough while Grace was home to be malicious, but Cindy was clearly aware enough to go there tonight.

Grace couldn't stay here anymore. She had to get out of the house and find somewhere else to stay for the next few days, even if it took every precious penny she'd saved. Believing she could come back here, even for two weeks, had been an epic mistake.

She blindly grabbed clean clothes and her bathroom clutch, shoving them in her briefcase. Quiet as possible, she pulled a textbook out of the closet. Flipping to the middle, she found the little section she'd cut away to create a small cubbyhole to store her emergency cash. She always kept enough for a bus ticket out of here plus incidentals, all the while knowing that if Cindy found it, she'd take it. Having that emergency stash had been the only way she could stay at her mother's house and not lose her mind. It had meant she wasn't trapped there. Not really. Still, her instincts urged her toward self-preservation they clearly identified as "escape."

Grace pocketed the small wad of cash and closed the lid, slipping the book back in place. Bracing herself, she opened her door, stepped over the broken glass and started for the front door.

"Where you goin' all dressed to the nines?" Cindy slurred. "Finally found yourself a man to unfreeze your frigid little ass?"

"I don't owe you an explanation."

"Don't disrespect me, Grace. I asked you a question."

Grace stopped and spun. "You're drunk. You won't remember tomorrow what you asked me tonight any more than you'll remember my answer, but I'll tell you, anyway. I'm going out. Away. As far from this hellhole as I can get. And yes, a man is involved."

Cindy laughed, the sound one of bitterness and disillusionment. "Here I was giving you flak about the man, and what do you do but admit you found someone to put up with your princess-and-the-pumpkin ideas about what happens between a man and a woman. You're a fool, Grace. An absolute fool. You think his interest in you is gonna last? You think he's gonna believe you're worth the trouble once he gets to know you?" When Grace didn't answer, Cindy snorted. "Fool."

Chest heaving, fury climbed Grace's spine one vertebra at a time, its vicious fingers piercing her emotional skin and leaving her bleeding. "Good night, Cindy."

Grace slammed the front door behind her. All she wanted was peace and quiet, a place she could retreat to after work and just relax. She didn't want to deal with her alcoholic mother. She didn't want to be hit on by her mother's lovers as they left Cindy's house. She didn't want to be afraid for one more night, didn't want to be rejected again.

She hated her mother for stealing her joy, for finding it funny when her revolving-door lovers flirted with Grace or, worse, had come into her room to tuck her in as a child.

A hard shiver shook her. She'd started sleeping with a steak knife at eight. She'd graduated to a butcher knife by eleven. Had pulled it on a man by thirteen. Had drawn blood by fourteen. And all the while, she'd held out a kernel of hope that love could defeat the darkness in her life. Her mother might have denied it to Grace over the course of her life, but Grace had always hoped someday she'd find someone who would love her freely. Someday she'd get out of Cindy's house and find a way to be happy. The woman was right. Grace had been a fool.

Choking on a toxic blend of loathing and self-pity, she stepped onto the 18 bus at the same time a gunshot sounded. The driver slammed the doors and started pulling away from the curb, leaving her to lurch toward the first empty seat. He drove faster than was legal, but still not fast enough for Grace.

She wanted out.

Now.

JUSTIN SWIVELED IN HIS chair and checked Pandora's front door yet again. It was almost 7:45 p.m. and Grace hadn't shown up. He turned back in time to see Eric and Levi exchange a knowing look. "What?" he demanded. "I'm worried she ran into trouble. This isn't the best neighborhood."

"It's the South Central District, Justin. She'll be fine. Probably just ran into someone she recognized outside a neighboring bar." Levi smiled innocently. "Maybe a frat guy or a professor or someone."

Justin grabbed a peanut and flicked it at the guy, beaning him in the forehead. "Shut up about Grace, Levi. I'm not telling you again."

"Man, you've got it bad," Eric said through a wide grin.

"Pot, kettle," Justin responded blandly before glancing at Cass. "No offense, beautiful."

"None taken. He could take being set down a peg or two." The woman at Eric's side then turned to her boyfriend and gently slapped the back of his head. "Now be nice. You have to chill out where Justin's concerned. So what if he has a girlfriend?"

"She's not my girlfriend." Justin had clarified this every time Grace entered the conversation, which had been often. "She's a girl who is my friend."

"Girlfriend," Cass insisted. "I have girlfriends. Why can't you?"

"Bring them over," Eric said, waggling his eyebrows.

Cass rolled her eyes. "You've got a one-track mind." She smiled brightly at Justin. "So. Why *isn't* she your girlfriend?"

Justin took a long draw from his beer. "It's complicated."

Levi settled deeper in his chair and stared a hole through Justin. "Dark auburn hair, right? Swimsuit-model physique but with better curves?"

"Hair's more red than auburn, but yeah, she's got killer curves. A little more on her than a swimsuit model, which makes her absolutely freakin' perfect. Why?"

"She just walked in."

Justin whipped around so fast he almost fell out of his chair.

And there she was, scanning the crowd as she chewed her bottom lip. She looked amazing in faded jeans and a sleeveless green top. He raised a hand to grab her attention, smiling when she started their way.

The closer she came, though, the clearer it became that something was wrong. The tell was in her eyes. They were haunted. Or hunted. Or both. She'd worried the lipstick off one half of her lower lip, and he was sure his friends would notice, maybe ask if she was okay. To save her any discomfort, he stood and stepped forward, quickly dropping a kiss on her lips with enough pressure to transfer her lipstick.

Her eyes widened and she parked a hand on his chest, pushing at him gently until he pulled away. "I've heard that hello is a generally accepted greeting in most countries, including ours."

"So trite, 'hello.' I thought I'd do something a bit more European."

"They air kiss on one or both cheeks."

"Middle Eastern?"

"Their women generally aren't allowed to show any forms of public affection."

"You're tough, Cooper. Caribbean."

"I haven't had enough rum to believe you're from the Caribbean, Maxwell."

"Then let's get the lady a drink."

She laughed, and the haunted look in her eyes retreated a few paces.

"Before you get mad about the kiss," he said into her ear, "you'd worried the lipstick off one side of your lower lip. I figured you wouldn't want anyone to ask what was wrong. A kiss seemed the most expedient way of resolving the issue. Unfortunately, you'll have to act like my date now or they're going to want to know why I kissed you at all."

Her smile slowly faded as she searched his face.

He bristled. "I don't go around kissing women, Grace."

Laying a hand gently on his cheek, she leaned forward and pulled him in for a very tender kiss.

Justin's heart did a lazy roll in his chest that left him breathless when she broke away.

Turning, he placed one hand at the small of her back and encouraged Grace forward. It amused him that both Eric and Levi stood after Cass unapologetically kicked them under the table.

Eric slipped an arm around Cass's shoulders. "This must be Grace Cooper."

"The one and only," Justin answered, nudging her forward another step and wondering at the fact the saucy wench he was crazy about had gone totally silent in the face of unknown men. Narrowing his eyes, he considered Eric and Levi objectively. They were both tall. Eric was leanly muscled, whereas Levi was bulkier, but not so huge his head seemed too small for his body. Both men sported dark hair, but Levi's was nearly black and hung to his shoulders while Eric's was executive chic all the way. Both were attractive, had great personalities. And suddenly he felt as if he was sizing his best friends up for dates versus assessing them for…what? Competition?

Levi shook his head, drawing Justin's attention. "If you don't stop looking at me like you're trying to decide whether or not to take me home, I'm going to either knock you on your ass or demand you at least buy me a drink first."

Everyone laughed, including Grace, so Justin went along with it. When he got Levi alone, though, they'd see who ended up on whose ass. For now, he dropped an arm around Grace's shoulders and said, "You're cute, but you're not my type."

"I'd rather be her type than yours, anyway." Levi waggled his brows.

Justin stiffened, but Grace just laughed and leaned forward, resting her forearms on the bar-height table. "The only thing that means, hotshot, is that you're going to go to bed wishing."

Grace settled into Justin's side as the group laughed again.

Levi lifted his beer in salute.

Cass pulled out a chair for Grace and said, "At first I was just glad you came because I'm tired of being the only woman in this group, but I think I'm going to really like you."

Something shifted inside Justin, something he hadn't expected. He'd wanted the people around this table to approve of Grace, and now he was sure they did. That only made him more determined than ever to gain her willingness to take a chance on him, to trust him, not just physically but emotionally.

The way she'd looked when she'd walked through the door said she'd given emotional control over to someone—the *wrong* someone. That person had stolen the color from her cheeks, robbed her of her confidence. He wanted to give it back to her.

Grace slid onto the stool Cass offered and fell into

easy conversation with the other woman. Something quiet moved through Justin. She was amazing. Brilliant. Beautiful. And he only knew one way to convince her what he was experiencing was absolute truth.

Stepping up to the chair, he slid his hand under Grace's mass of hair and gripped her neck, angling her face toward him even as he leaned into her. He didn't ask for permission. He didn't offer excuses. He wanted her to know how desperate he was for her, how incredible she was to him.

There were teeth and tongues and short breaths, all mingling as he struggled to offer her some measure of selflessness. Because in the midst of the kiss, one thing had become crystal clear to Justin.

Grace Cooper was the woman for him.

13

GRACE BARELY REMEMBERED to breathe. Justin's kiss did that to her. Part of her wanted to protest and demand he stop, but that voice was so tiny compared to the singular chorus of "Yes!" every other part of her was singing.

Heat flooded her pelvis and she swiveled to face him, opening her legs to settle him between her thighs. Her hands framed his face to offer far more support than direction. She wasn't sure he noticed.

His tongue plundered her mouth, aggressive and demanding.

She sighed, relaxing and letting him control the moment entirely. Giving up control was an experience in itself, one that left her craving his control in a more intimate way. She suddenly wanted it all from him, and maybe that was wrong. She wasn't sure. All she knew for certain was that the man in her arms burned as hot for her as she did for him. And that's what she'd needed tonight.

He broke the kiss and rested his forehead against hers, his hands on the upper swells of her hips. "Hi."

Her voice evaded her. She cleared her throat and then coughed. "We went over this greeting thing you've got going on, Dr. Maxwell."

"We did. I wondered if you'd remember."

"It was fifteen minutes ago. Did we ever decide who greets like this?"

"I believe it was decided we do."

She fought not to smile and failed. "I don't remember agreeing to that."

"You didn't. I decided for us." Justin glanced at Cass. "Give us a minute?"

"Gentlemen, I need a drink from the bar and it's going to take all three of us to get it. Move that fine ass, Levi," she sing-songed when he lagged behind.

Alone, Justin faced Grace. "I want you."

Eyes sparkling, she cocked her head. "Seems like a very public venue. Wait. Don't tell me. You're secretly an exhibitionist who's been waiting to come out to his friends, and I'm just the girl to help you do it."

"Well, I *am* a stripper…" He traced a thumb along her jaw. "No. No jokes."

Her brow furrowed as her smile faded. Confusion fogged her mind. "I don't get what you're after here."

"I want you, Grace. That's no secret. What if we tried exclusivity?"

"Exclusivity," she parroted through lips gone numb.

"Yeah." He traced a finger down her neck to her collarbone, leaving a blazing trail against her skin. "You know—you plus me equals us."

Stunned, she said the only thing she could say. "This is fun, Justin. I'll give you that. But there is no 'us.'"

"There could be."

Her heart ached at the sincerity in his voice, and she suddenly regretted coming out tonight. She'd just said she wanted this, wanted someone to offer her refuge—but it couldn't be him. She refused to stay in Seattle, and he wouldn't leave.

So she'd keep him at arm's length. There might be a few kisses and such, but there wouldn't be anything more.

After the scene with her mother, she wanted nothing more than to crawl into his arms and stay there forever—nothing more than to run as fast as possible from the emotional wasteland she'd been born into.

Angry tears burned the back of her throat and forced her to swallow them down. Shaking her head, she looked up at him, allowing herself the momentary luxury of being able to touch him without apologies or fear.

So why let this go? her conscious whispered. *When has anyone ever offered you a couple of weeks of unmitigated happy?*

Impulsiveness crashed into her like a twenty-car pileup. It didn't have to be a choice. She could seize the moment, take what he offered, give what she could in return and then go. All she had to do was take a page from his book and set ground rules for the days they would spend together. "If you want to have a little fun over the next couple of weeks, that's great. But after that? I'm gone. I have to make a clean break, get out and start living, start fresh. I can't do that in Seattle."

A fine tremor ran through him, crossing every point of contact between them. "A little fun for a couple of weeks, huh?"

"You make it sound unappealing. That's not the way I meant it," she said, hurt warring with anger in both her voice and heart. "That's not fair."

"What's not 'fair' is you taking my offer of something more and twisting it around. I won't settle, Grace. Not for less than what I deserve."

"Deserve, huh? And you deserve more than me. Nice." She stood and grabbed her messenger bag.

"Uh-uh. You don't walk out on me a second time."

"This isn't like before. This time I'm walking out on you for good, Justin." She started for the door, irritated when he followed her. Spinning, she slapped a hand against his chest. "Cut it out. I'm not into causing scenes."

"Stay. Argue with me, Grace. We're worth it. Please."

The plea sliced through her like piano wire through skin—efficient and painful. "Justin—"

"I'm not above begging. It's just…" He swallowed hard. "I don't want less than a real shot, Grace."

She arched a brow. "What about the 'I'm not settling' diatribe you loosed on me seconds ago?"

He reached out and took her hand, and a small jolt of awareness made her eyes snap to his. "I would never consider a relationship with you to be 'settling.' Give me two weeks to convince you this thing between us is worth trying."

"You have nine days, and no promises. My friend Meg called just before I got here. She passed my résumé on to her new boss in Baltimore. They're interested. If the opportunity is there, I'm going to take it."

He gave a stiff, hard nod. "Fine. Nine days."

"And if it doesn't work out, I don't want to lose your friendship. Promise me that, Justin."

"All I can promise is that I'll do my best to honor your request," he said softly. "But if you break my heart? It might be a while before I'm up for sitting down to chat over coffee."

If you break my heart. Her stomach plummeted, achieving terminal velocity in record time considering she was five-nine. She didn't want to hurt him, had never in a million years considered she might be in a position where she could. How quickly things changed. The one constant was that she wanted him. Badly. And this might be her only chance to have him. Holding on to that thread of impulsiveness that was fast fading, she looked up and nodded. "I understand."

"So you'll give me nine days to…" He trailed off, clearly waiting for her to finish the sentence.

Her hand went to her throat, gently massaging the tightness that threatened to strangle her. *How to finish that sentence?* Too many options, but only one real answer. If nothing else, Grace wanted a piece of happy. She wanted moments to look back on that colored the start of her life in brilliant swaths, not the dismal grays and blacks of the life she'd been born into.

Her gaze locked on his. "I'll give you nine days to convince me that giving this thing a shot is worth the risk."

And that was it, right there. *The risk.* So many things could go wrong, so much could happen that would make this thing between them pull a Hindenburg and go up in spectacular flames.

She wouldn't think about that last, though. As long as she maintained her sanity while Justin—she swallowed hard—pursued her, she'd be able to ensure nobody got hurt in the end. And it *would* end.

Still, the idea of him pursuing her was so ludicrous after the past three years that she couldn't help but smile.

"What?" he asked, automatically smiling in return.

"Did you ever think we'd find ourselves here?"

"Here?"

"You know." She waggled a hand between them. "Here. With you trying to get me to give this a shot?"

"No, but I'm damn glad we're standing where we are."

"Why?"

"Because I've stared at you for years, Grace. I've been hungry for the sound of your laugh. It makes me feel a hundred feet tall. Invincible, even. Because I've wanted to know what you think about in the middle of night when you can't sleep." He stepped toward her and slid a hand around her waist, encouraging her to step in to his body. "Because I love the way you fit in my arms." He lowered his lips to brush over hers as he spoke. "Because I love the way your lips feel against mine."

He traced the seam of her lips with his tongue until she opened to him. Then he kissed her. Thoroughly. Breaking away, he ran his free hand through her hair and gripped her head, forcing her to continue to look at him. "Because I love the way you taste."

"That's a lot of—" she nearly choked "—love."

"Yeah," he said softly. "It is."

Knowing he was falling for her scared her to death. She'd agreed to the next nine days believing she could pull it off without anybody getting hurt. But was that possible knowing he was already so invested?

What had she just done?

JUSTIN WANTED TO loose a triumphant shout...right after he threw up. He'd managed to get her to agree to give him nine days—and he fully intended to make the most of every second to show her how much she could be loved. That last was the vomit inducer. *Love.* He'd been crazy about her for years, but love? That took time, intimate time, they didn't have. The most he could do was set them on the right path and hope she recognized it.

Guiding her to the table, he took her bag, surprised at the weight. "What have you got in here? Hockey gear?"

"Change of clothes. It takes a lot to be a proper woman," she said primly.

"Lord knows that's right," Cass added, slipping into the chair beside Grace and sliding a drink her way. "I thought you might want this."

Justin watched the emotions play across Grace's face before she responded. "Thanks. I, um, I don't drink."

"My bad." Cass slid the drink to her place and stared at it, frowning. "It's frozen, which means I have to drink both it and mine." She looked up, grinning. "Unless Levi wants it."

"Are you insane?" the man asked, indignant. "I drink a girly drink like that and I'll grow breasts."

"Just think, man," Eric said with a wicked grin. "You could stay home and play with your own pair instead of having to find a new set every night."

Levi chucked the lemon from his drink at Eric and grinned. "Yeah, but I like to play with other parts of a woman, too. I'll pass."

"Fine." Cass sighed before taking a long pull on her straw, sucking down a good bit of her daiquiri. "Oh! Oh, crap! Brain freeze!"

Everyone laughed as she gripped her head and alternated between cursing and laughter.

The band for the evening was just setting up, tuning instruments and synching the sound system to prevent the squelch of feedback that had people shouting their disapproval. They succeeded in the former but missed the latter by a mile.

Justin dropped an arm around Grace's shoulders, pulling her close.

"Who's playing tonight?" she asked as she snuggled into his side.

He rubbed his nose and tried not to laugh. "The chalkboard marquee outside called them something like 'Humping Monkeys.'"

"Humpday Monkeys, you idiot." Levi tossed the last of his drink down his throat. "Hump*day*, as in middle of the week. How is it you're the smartest one in the group when you can't even read?"

"Easy there, gorilla boy," Grace snapped. "He's a psychologist, not a zoologist."

Levi stared at her, mouth hanging open.

Justin half wondered if he was going to have to break up

a verbal smackdown because, though many weren't aware of it, Levi was highly educated and a bit sensitive about it.

The other man shook his head. "Gorilla boy?"

She arched a single brow. "Just be glad I didn't get into their penchant for picking fleas."

"I usually reserve that pleasurable activity for those closest to me, and right now? You're closest." Levi lunged for her and she squealed, scrambling behind Justin. The dark-haired man settled back in his seat, laughter lighting up his face. "Never pick a fight with someone you can't win against."

"I've got Justin."

Levi chuckled. "And you think the good doctor can take me down?"

Justin watched the entire interchange with a growing sense of doom. "No need to embarrass Levi, is there?"

"Nice try, Professor," Grace said on a smile. Turning back to Levi, she slipped her arm around Justin's waist.

His chest tightened. It was the first time she'd initiated contact just for the sake of contact. Not in a sexual way, not in response to something he'd done. She'd just touched him for the sake of touching.

She leaned forward. "Let me see your hands."

Levi's brows drew together but he held out a hand.

Inspecting it carefully, she looked up at Justin and nodded. The amusement in her gaze stole the last of his breath. "Grace."

"Five bucks and a beer says the professor here can take you at thumb wrestling. One match, elbows stay on the table, no broken digits, play till one of you is pinned."

"And whoever wins gets a kiss from you," Levi added.

Justin glared, his fists tightening.

"Deal," Grace said.

Justin sputtered, unable to find the words to protest.

"You had me at the free beer." Levi rolled his sleeve

up, flexing his fingers. "The kiss was just to make the professor Hulk out. He's usually the calmest in the group, so this is a treat."

Justin looked down at her. "A thumb-wrestling death match?"

"Don't lose," she muttered. "I'm *not* buying that free-range gorilla a beer. He'd ask for a pitcher. And I'm *not* kissing him."

Justin couldn't help it. He laughed, long and loud, even as he rolled one sleeve up. "Best reason there is not to lose. Then I'd have to kill the guy, and that would just be awkward."

He settled his elbow on the table and squared off with Levi. Their joking and laughing had drawn attention, and a small crowd gathered around the table.

"Thumb wrestling?" someone murmured.

"Ten says brown hair takes black hair."

"You're on. Black hair has some serious muscle going on."

Conversation buzzed around them, and Justin found himself unable to stop the smile that had been flirting with the corners of his mouth. "We're going to get arrested for betting on a sporting event."

"It was a long, extraordinarily harsh winter, yes, but to get this worked up over thumb wrestling?" Levi muttered, shaking his head. "People should get out more."

"On three," a stranger called. "One…two…three!"

Justin watched Levi's strategy. Composed of brute strength, his obvious intent was to pin Justin's thumb and hold it there to another count of three. Justin toyed with him a little, teasing, letting Levi almost capture his thumb and then he struck. Levi broke the hold and the crowd cheered and groaned in equal measure. Letting Levi build his confidence back to dangerously high levels, Justin struck again, this time relaxing his hand for a fraction of a second and retightening it, depressing Levi's thumb so it was bent at a painful angle.

"One…two…three!" the crowd shouted before a rousing cheer went up.

Levi dug out his wallet and handed Grace a five-dollar bill before tipping an imaginary hat in her direction. "How could you be sure he'd win?"

"I wasn't." Grace shrugged. "But he has bigger hands and is unbelievably skilled with them." She winked at Levi even as the other man roared with laughter. "Besides, when you threw in the kiss? I was sure he'd want to collect."

"Too right." He glanced at Levi. "She's off-limits."

"Man, I wouldn't have kissed her."

"Something wrong with me?" Grace demanded, crossing her arms under her breasts.

"Not a damn thing, sweetheart." Levi grew serious and Justin worried about what the man might say.

He should have known to trust him.

Cupping Grace's jaw, he kissed her gently on the forehead. "You're the professor's. That much is obvious. And while I might be the bigger of the two of us, I'm not about to pit myself against him where you're involved. He'd snap me in half in order to preserve your honor."

Justin turned Grace to face him. "I believe a kiss from you is part of the prize pack."

"Well, a kiss and a beer." She shrugged. "Plus I'll split my five bucks with you."

"Keep the five bucks and buy me a beer this weekend. For now? I just want my kiss."

The way she eyed him so suspiciously reminded him that his goal was to earn her trust, to prove he was more than a one-night stand that culminated in a few poorly chosen words. He wanted her to be assured that he wanted *her*, not sex. Well, not only sex.

Bending low, he hoisted her over his shoulder in a fireman's carry, slapping her ass when she squealed in protest.

"Put me down right now, Justin Maxwell!"

"Hey, isn't that the guy from Beaux Hommes?" a woman nearby asked.

Just for tonight, they could all go to hell—all the fans, the regulars who knew him, the bouncers who eyed him suspiciously, his friends who were watching with renewed interest. Tonight was about Grace. He was going to show her exactly what he was made of.

"Someone sacrifice their keys," he said, holding out a hand and wiggling his fingers. "We'll be back in a little while."

"Take my truck." Cass dug out her keys and tossed them to him.

Justin moved toward the door and the crowd parted like he was Moses headed for the Promised Land.

He considered the woman in his arms and decided that, in a way, he was.

14

"I CAN'T BREATHE," Grace protested, pushing up from Justin's lower back.

"Yikes, woman. *Kidneys*. A man has *kidneys*."

"Well, put me down."

"Nope." He adjusted his hold, putting more pressure on her hips rather than the soft part of her belly. "I'd rather piss blood."

"Pretty picture." She watched his ass flex as he walked, trying not to think about the people gaping at them as they passed. A wicked thought crowded her mind. Letting herself down on her hips, she arched her back, curled her fingers and dug them into Justin's sides. "Oomph!"

He jumped, knocking the wind out of her and twisting his torso wildly to get away from her hands. "Cut it out, Grace!" he shouted, laughing.

"*Ovaries*, Justin. A woman has *ovaries*."

He carried her through the doors to the parking lot. Cool air heavy with mist settled around her, tracing invisible fingers around her waist where her shirt had lifted and exposed skin. She shivered.

"Cass's car should be nearby. Look for a dark truck that says *Preservations* on the side."

"All I can see is your butt. Don't get me wrong—it's a great view. But that leaves me pretty useless when it comes to helping you find the truck, unless you happen to be walking away from it."

He snorted, pulling her forward and casually hooking one arm behind her knees and the other around her shoulders.

Something decidedly feminine in her fluttered at being handled so easily. Good Lord, she could be such a girl sometimes.

"There." Justin shifted her just enough that he could beep the gleaming truck open. "She didn't mention she'd bought a new truck."

"Nice, though I'm more an Audi A8-S girl."

"An import girl after my own heart." He grinned, shifting her again, this time to open the door and carefully set her down so she was seated but facing out. He saw her settled before gently maneuvering his way in between her thighs.

Flustered, she glanced up into his face. "What are we doing out here?"

Work-roughened fingertips traced down her neck and settled over her erratic heartbeat. "Nothing."

"Clearly our definitions of *nothing* are different." She leaned against the passenger seat. "Awful lot of work to go through to collect on a kiss."

"Not really." He shrugged, broad shoulders briefly blocking the streetlight. "Besides, I'm saving the kiss."

Her guard went up. "For what?"

"Such skepticism, Grace. Just saving it."

"Then why the big to-do about carrying me out of the bar?"

"Did it bug you?"

"No." The admission proved harder than it should have.

"Why not?"

"I suppose every woman wants to feel a little feminine

now and again, and strong men do that to us." She pushed at her hair and fought a shiver.

"Jeez. I'm sorry. I didn't even think about you being cold. Watch your fingers," he warned before slamming the truck door.

He jogged around to the driver's side and hopped in, cranked the engine and punched up the heat. "Should have heated seats," he murmured, tracing his fingers over the dashboard. "Aha!"

"Why should it have heated seats?"

Justin punched a pair of buttons and the seats started to warm. "Cass has busted her tail to carve out a place in the engineering world, and heated seats are her way of saying she's made it."

Grace grinned. "The more I learn about Cass, the more I find I could quickly grow fond of her."

Justin answered her grin with one of his own. "Eric feels the same way."

"How long have they been together?"

Justin leaned his seat back and rested his hands on his stomach. "Oh, about six months. They're good for each other," he added softly. "It's nice to see him happy."

Twisting in her seat, Grace tucked her legs up under her and leaned against the passenger door. Watching Justin like this, still and relaxed, was a surprising treat. She hadn't realized how he was always in motion. Not until he stopped. Now, with the light glinting off his hair, his capable hands at rest over his abs and his eyes closed, he appeared relaxed in a way she hadn't witnessed, even at the diner.

"If you don't stop staring at me, I'm going to develop a complex." His smooth voice slid over her, through her, leaving goose bumps in its wake.

"Yeah? Well, lucky for you, I'm qualified to diagnose all manner of complexes." She leaned forward, propping her forearms on the console. "So tell me, Dr. Maxwell, what's the root of your complex? Your past? Your present? What you want in your future? Hopes? Dreams? Disappointments?"

He rolled his head toward her but didn't open his eyes. "You should be required to license your voice."

"What? Why?"

"Dangerously seductive weapon, that." Then he was quiet for so long she wondered if he'd actually dozed off. Then he answered. "Come here, Grace."

She didn't think—she simply crawled into his arms after he folded the console back and reached for her. The warmth of his skin bled through her shirt. A deep sigh escaped her. "You feel good."

"Ditto." He brushed his lips over the crown of her head. "Why were you upset earlier tonight?"

She fought not to stiffen in his arms and failed. Miserably. "As of tonight, I'm homeless."

"Excuse me?" His voice was low and calm, yet hard enough to sound dangerous in the darkness.

Fine tremors started in her hands, spreading up her arms to coalesce in her shoulders, forming knotted masses of tension. "I had to leave my mom's house."

His voice dropped lower. "Why?"

Why? "Because I pulled the unforgivable and ruined her life, too."

"Exactly how did you ruin her life?" If she'd thought his voice hard before, it was now absolutely dangerous, filled with darkness and fury.

Her throat tightened and she wheezed the answer. "I was born."

"Oh, hell, Grace. I'm sorry I ever said you might ruin my life."

She shook her head and tried to swallow.

"You're amazing, the best thing that's ever happened to

me, and you're safe with me, baby." His voice, now even lower, sounded as if it were being scraped over gravel, raw and pained.

That heartfelt message, coming on the heels of fleeing her mother's house and the friendships she'd encountered in the bar—it was all too much. Pushing out of his arms, she scrambled to the passenger door and out of the truck. Her breath sawed in and out of her lungs. Tears burned her eyes, her vision blurring as she fought to simply claim enough air to keep from passing out. She wanted to run, but had absolutely nowhere to go. The realization was a crippling blow. Every effort to draw a breath failed. Black dots danced through her vision and she thought she might pass out for the first time in her life.

A car door slammed. Feet crunched on gravel, coming closer.

She had to save herself from this mess, had to find a way to get through the next nine days and not collapse. Her only choice was the women's shelter or the YMC—

Strong arms wordlessly hauled her into a hard body.

She turned into the embrace that was more and more familiar, found the promised safety in those arms, and the permission to simply be. No pressure, no expectations, no need to fight to survive, no fear of rejection. He was her safe harbor. She clung to him as she was battered by wave after wave of emotion.

Whispered words broke through the battlements of her madness, words that soothed her fears. She struggled to hear him and not to give in to the grief that threatened to rip her apart. In the end, she didn't have a choice.

The first sob was wrenched from the very heart of her, the sound more a broken groan than a wail. Tears streamed down her face as she sagged in those strong arms, arms that embraced her, supported her.

Hot tears scalded her cheeks, and her whole body shook with their release.

"Let it go, baby. I've got you."

Those last three words untied the final knot of hesitation. She held on and did just as he'd advised.

She let it go.

JUSTIN HAD NO CLUE HOW they'd gone from thumb wrestling for beer and kisses thirty minutes ago to Grace having an emotional breakdown in his arms. Several things were certain, though. First, Grace came from a background of hardship and heartache, and he wanted to show her she deserved so much more.

Second, he wanted to kill Grace's mother. An age-old need to do violence rushed through his veins, a kind of drug he'd long forgotten but still recognized and, at the moment, craved. He'd fought for years to master his emotions, was famed for his control, and now that control broke. He shook with the urge to cause that woman unspeakable harm. It thrilled him as much as it scared him. He could destroy her and none would be the wiser.

But for Grace, he would stem his violence, would control himself and refuse to fall into that vast blackness that called to him, his own personal siren's song. Grace was worth the sacrifice he'd make to do the right thing, not the thing he most wanted to do.

Third, he was going to be her safety and security. No matter the cost, he would provide a safe haven for her. Period. He was so grateful the arms she'd fled to had been his. She was stronger than she believed herself to be, and smart enough to fend for herself. But she'd be stronger with him by her side. Only him. He would love her harder than anyone had ever been loved.

Everything inside him stilled. There it was again, that word. *Love.* What he'd thought he'd known of it, what he'd anticipated it would feel like—he threw it all out and held on to what he now understood love was. It was this woman in his arms, his own amazing Grace.

Murmuring words of encouragement, words to make her understand she was safe and cherished and loved, he gently moved her toward the pickup and searched with one hand until he found the tailgate latch. Letting it down, he eased his way onto the tailgate and pulled her with him, letting her curl up in his lap.

"Don't let go." She hiccupped the whispered plea between harsh breaths.

"Never, Grace," he whispered into her hair. "Never."

"I have nowhere to go." Her voice betrayed her broken spirit, and it slayed him as effectively as if she'd run him through with a sword.

He stroked her hair, thinking through his next words carefully. "You have me, baby. I want to ask you to do me a huge favor, one I understand goes against everything you've been taught."

She buried her face in his shirt and gave a pained laugh. "At this point? Anything."

The first note of hope rang through him. "I'm going to hold you to that. I'm going to go inside, call a cab and we're going back to my place. It's…rough, but it's safe and secure."

"Why would you do that for me?"

He lifted her chin and waited until she looked up at him. "Because I care about you. I didn't start to live until you came into the club. Before then, I breathed, my heart beat, my pulse registered. I was alive but I wasn't living. Not until you."

He'd been waiting, always waiting, for life to get on with it. He'd worked so hard for so long, and he'd always hoped there was more to it than eighty-hour workweeks, sleepless nights cramming for exams and crashing on his mother's sofa. And then Grace had sat in his class. The first time she'd smiled at him, the first time she'd challenged him, that's when his life started. And over the past three days, she'd shown him the waiting had been worth it.

He'd fallen in love.

He leaned forward, never closing his eyes, never breaking away from her wide-eyed stare, and gently laid his lips to hers. This was a kiss meant to heal old hurts and build new foundations. It was a moment between them, a covenant of truth that would hold and never be forgotten.

Her lips were soft, her response tentative.

He persisted, never pushing but never giving up the ground he'd made. She had to know he could be strong enough for the two of them.

When she finally began to respond, he kept things slow, almost lazy, despite the burning need he had to lay her down and love her senseless. There would be time for that. For now? This was the most he would do. He'd show her in every way he could imagine that he loved her madly, passionately, thoroughly and wholly. And when the moment was right, when she'd found her footing again, he'd give her the words.

Breaking away, he cupped her face. "If that doesn't convey the fact you didn't ruin my life, you'll just have to stick around until I can find a way to better explain it."

Ageless eyes peered at him, the sheen of tears she wasn't quite done shedding reflecting in the lamplight. "I could get used to that."

He gave a short nod. "I want you to wait here. I'll be back in just a second, okay?"

"Okay."

"Don't leave." He had this fear her first instinct would be to run the minute he was gone. "Please."

"I promise I'll wait." Her gaze dropped to her hands

twisting in her lap. "Sorry I fell apart. I normally handle life better than this."

"Hey. No one can take years of verbal abuse and come out unscathed. You should know that, Grace."

"Right. I just…" She bit the inside of her cheek. "I thought I had more control over it until she blew up at me tonight."

"You haven't lived at home while you were in school, right?"

She shook her head. "No. I wouldn't have survived. I lived with my friend, Meg, at a place she co-opted from a guy, a doctor, who'd been working abroad. The guy came home early, no notice, so we were in the apartment one night and out the next. My mom's place was the cheapest option, and I figured I could manage it for two weeks."

One statement stuck out blatantly. "You say you wouldn't have survived. Why?"

"No therapy, okay?"

He reached over and took her hands in his, giving them a gentle squeeze. "No therapy. I'm just trying to put the pieces together."

"My mom has a house on Aurora Boulevard, commonly known as Drive-By Boulevard."

His stomach pitched, and he squeezed her hands a little too hard before realizing what he was doing. Relaxing his grip, he lifted her fingers to his mouth and kissed each knuckle. "I'm sorry you had to grow up in such a bad environment."

Grace shifted to rest her cheek against his chest and over his heart. "That's a nice way to say, 'Hey, sorry you grew up in the slums.'"

Justin held her, let her breathe for a few minutes as he ran his fingers through her hair and laid small kisses to any part of her he could reach without moving her. Finally, when her breathing calmed, he took her shoulders and helped her sit up. "I have to get Cass's keys back to her. I'll drop them off and call a cab, okay?"

"The bus would be cheaper."

"It would, but a cab is far more private. You've been crying and people are rudely curious. They'd stare. It's also why I'm asking you to stay out here while I go inside. I don't want anyone asking you questions you don't want to answer."

Wrapping a hand around the back of his neck, she pulled him in for the sweetest kiss. "Thank you. I never knew my knight in shining armor would show up not on a horse but in a black and yellow."

Justin smiled. "There's the woman I…recognize." Fighting to regain his equilibrium, he hopped off the tailgate. "Sit tight."

It took every ounce of control not to sprint into the bar. He compromised by jogging. Quickly.

Once inside, he found Eric and Cass at the table. "Where's Levi?"

Eric jerked his chin to the right. "Playing pool with a leggy blonde. Never thought I'd say this, but I doubt he's going to go home with her. Something's going on with him. He's acting strange."

Loyalty made Justin want to dig into it and help out. Love made him hand the keys over and say, "I'm taking Grace to my place tonight. Do *not* comment, my friend," he interjected when Eric opened his mouth. "It's not like that. She needs someplace quiet."

Cass's brows drew together. "Everything okay?"

He shoved his hands in his pockets. "It will be."

"We won't push," Eric said as he took Cass's hand. "We've been there, we understand how hard it can be to sort out priorities and shit at the beginning of a relationship."

"I love her," Justin blurted. "And I have *no* idea why I just told you that."

Cass reached over with her free hand and squeezed Justin's wrist. "Because love, as grand as it is, can be a burden. And sometimes you just need someone else to help carry the load."

His throat tightened and he nodded. "Yeah."

"Take my car if you want a ride." Eric began to dig in his pocket for his keys.

"That would be great." He accepted the proffered key fob and stared at it until he was able to harness his emotions. "Thanks. I'll return it tomorrow, first thing."

"He can stay with me and we'll commute together, so keep it as long as necessary." Cass looked at Eric. "I just gave away your car, babe. Sorry."

Eric grinned softly. "Would've done it myself, but you beat me to it." He nodded to Justin. "Go."

"Yeah." Spinning on his heel, Justin strode to the door, outside and straight to the truck.

Life was waiting.

15

JUSTIN TOSSED HER BAG in the back of a modest sedan before handing Grace into the passenger seat as if she'd been made of superfine porcelain. "Eric's car. No black and yellow tonight."

"Did you say anything? About me?" The last thing she wanted were his friends believing she was as fragile as she felt.

"Only that I was taking you to my place. Let 'em infer what they will." He started the car and glanced over. "That okay with you?"

"Better than the alternative."

His brow had creased. "What do you mean?"

"Telling them that you managed to ask the one question I couldn't answer without falling apart." She sighed. "Not true. None of this is your fault." And just when she thought she was out of tears, her chest tightened. "I don't want them to assume—"

"They won't," he interjected, the severity of his words harsh enough to stem further conversation, so she let it go.

The ride to his apartment was comforting in that it was absolutely silent. Justin seemed to realize Grace didn't want to talk and for that she was grateful. Honestly, she couldn't look at him and be ungrateful about much of anything. He'd hurt her, yes. But she accepted that he was truly sorry for his words. He wouldn't fake the level of sincerity he'd shown tonight. Justin wasn't that kind of man.

They approached his complex with much less desperation than they'd approached the hotel Saturday night. No racing to the curb, or racing from the car, or racing to the room. Following the earlier emotional purge, it seemed almost anticlimactic. She was so lethargic her limbs felt as if they'd been cast in concrete. The light from oncoming traffic made her eyes burn. Leaning her head against the headrest, she let her mind go where it would.

She was peripherally surprised fear no longer owned her. Left in its wake was a muted sense of acceptance, a realization that she had made the irrevocable break from the life she'd led until the moment she'd come apart. Putting herself together again would happen more slowly as she figured out who she wanted to be.

She didn't open her eyes when Justin stroked her hair. Instead, she blindly held out a hand. He took what she offered, holding it tenderly. That was so representative of who he was, that he would wordlessly cradle the piece of her she offered. How had it taken her so long to realize what a remarkable man he was? How had she been so blind where he was concerned?

"My place is on the second floor. I have no idea how quiet it is on the weekends. I've only had it a few weeks and it's…Spartan? That might be an understatement. But I finally bought a bed and I—"

"You don't owe me an explanation," she whispered. "But I do want you to know I'm sorry."

"Sorry? For what?" He pulled into the parking garage.

"I was so hard on you."

He took the first spot they came to, shutting the car off before shifting in his seat to face her. "What happened before? I own that. I was an ass. Period. You deserved, *de-*

serve, better than that. I intend to see you get it." He took her hand and held it over her heart. "From me."

"I have to say this." She swallowed that ever-familiar swell of emotion that made her breath come short. "What you said to me Saturday night? It hit every hot button I had. But now I feel like I have a clean slate—no past disappointments, no current expectations, no future dreams."

"That will change." He curled his fingers around hers and squeezed gently. "I promise."

She tried to smile but was sure simply it came off as a tired best effort. "Is that a promise from Justin Maxwell or Dr. Justin Maxwell?"

"Both." Leaning across the console, he unbuckled her seat belt. "Hang tight." He hopped out of the car and came to her door, helping her out.

When he bent low as if to pick her up, she backed up a step. "You can't carry me into the lobby."

He met her gaze and grinned. "Just picking up your bag, Ms. Cooper."

A faint blush warmed her cheeks. "Fair enough. Remind me to tip you when we get to the room. I won five bucks off a chump earlier."

Justin snorted. "He'll never hear the end of that. I promise."

Leaning on him for support, she let him lead her across the street, through the lobby and into the elevator. Memories of their first elevator ride together warmed her. He'd held her bag then, too.

When the elevator announced their arrival at the second floor, Justin guided her out. He made to open the door and froze, looking at her with almost bashful chagrin.

"What?" she asked, swaying with exhaustion when he took his arm away to adjust his hold on her bag.

Rolling his shoulders, he took a deep breath. "It's a one-bedroom apartment. I'm not so presumptuous as to believe we'd sleep together tonight, but I don't want to leave you alone."

She leaned one shoulder against the door frame. "I never assumed you'd drop me off and leave, and getting another hotel room isn't practical."

"It's important to me for you to really get that I only want what's in your best interest."

Again with that sincerity. She was too tired to think. Large capable hands wrapped around her upper arm, jolting her awake. Blinking rapidly, she gave a rueful smile. "I've got to lie down."

"Yeah, you should." He opened the door and helped her inside.

They entered through a tiny kitchen and went straight to an equally tiny bedroom. There were no furnishings save for the bed. Sinking onto the foot of the mattress, she watched him deposit her things in the closet before facing her. "You're going to be okay, Grace."

"I hope so." She sighed, the whoosh of breath shaky and shallow.

"You will. You're strong and smart and resilient. You're clearly a survivor. You're also a damn good agent to have if I ever go pro at thumb wrestling." He came to her then, pulling her heels off and setting them aside. Kneeling at her feet, he looked up, blue eyes clear. "How much help do you want getting ready for bed?"

"I could probably use your help getting undressed. My fingers aren't working quite right at the moment."

He sucked in a breath but instead of commenting, simply set to divesting her of her shirt and jeans before hesitating. "Did you bring pajamas?"

"I have no idea what I brought. I'm sure the clothes I wore today are in there because I changed on my way to the bar. There might be a couple other work outfits and a couple of T-shirts." She glanced up, mildly mortified. "I may have forgotten to include underwear for tomorrow."

His mouth opened and closed, but no sound escaped until he cleared his throat. "I'm not even sure what to do with that."

She smiled, this time more genuine than earlier. "I'll go to the nearest T.J. Maxx after work tomorrow."

"Fair enough." He dropped his gaze to the floor and ran a hand behind his neck, pulling hard enough his muscles shook. "So...no pajamas."

"No pajamas," she whispered.

"Grace, I can't... That is... Shit." He stood and spun away from her, leaning both hands against the nearest wall. "I can't help but be wickedly aroused. I'm a freaking lecher for reacting like this now of all times, but my body refuses to behave."

"Come here."

"I'm sorry, I simply can't get it to stand down—"

Mustering the last of her energy, she snapped, "Justin."

He gave her his profile but wouldn't face her. "What?"

"Come. Here." She patted the space beside her. "I'm cold."

The way he moved toward her, as if she might explode, amused her. The bulge in the front of his pants? She wished like mad she had the ability to take care of it. She was just so damn tired. He stopped in front of her, pulled his shirt over his head and gave it to her. It was warm and smelled of him, but she was so mesmerized by his hard body all she could do was hold the shirt in her limp hands.

"Help me up?" she asked. He did, pulling her to her feet. "Thanks." She turned, pulling her hair over her shoulder. "Would you please unhook my bra?"

Trembling fingers brushed over her skin, her nerves igniting every time he touched her.

"Sweet bleeding hell," he murmured when she let her bra fall to the floor and then kicked her underwear away.

She shrugged into the shirt, inhaling his scent off the fabric. "I'm cold, I'm more exhausted than I've ever been and I want to sleep for days, but not alone. Will you hold me?"

"Yeah." His one-word answer was so choked she would have laughed in almost any other situation.

He moved around her, folding the covers back on one side of the bed, and helped her in. Then he lay down on top of the comforter.

"What in the world are you doing?" she asked through a yawn.

"I was going to hold you until you fell asleep then move to the floor."

"I want to be held, Justin. *Held*. Ditch however many clothes you're comfortable with and crawl in."

Without a word, he rose and stripped in seconds. All the way to the skin. Folding down the covers on his side of the bed, he slid in and rolled toward her, pulling her into his arms and adjusting their positions until he was comfortably spooning her.

The last thing she remembered was him slipping one arm under her head and the other around her waist, snaking his hand between her breasts and hooking it over her far shoulder. "Sleep, baby. I've got you."

Then the world disappeared.

JUSTIN LAY AWAKE for two days. At least it *felt* like two days. It was probably only two hours. He held Grace close to his chest, listening to her breathe, feeling her heart beat beneath his wrist. The arm lying under her head began to go numb. Oh well. The pins and needles would suck in the morning, but they'd be worth every bit of discomfort because they meant he'd held her.

Nuzzling her hair, he was thrilled when she moved but less thrilled with *how* she moved. She snuggled even closer, the shirt riding up so that her bare backside rubbed against his aching shaft. Yeah, he'd been hard since he took off her shoes. Not a proud moment, that. Guilt had screamed at him to get himself under control, but he hadn't been able to even remotely deter the single-minded other piece of him that was shouting, "Yay! Naked Grace!" And now, every time he moved away from her, she followed his retreat so they were still pressed together.

This was going to be the longest night of his life.

She wiggled a little, getting comfortable, and he couldn't contain the soft hiss that escaped. "Get a grip, Maxwell."

"Justin?"

He stilled. "Yeah?"

"It's okay you're poking me in the back, but you've got to stop squirming."

He laughed softly, moving to prop himself up on one arm so he looked down at her. "Might help if you weren't so damn beautiful."

"You're biased. I wowed you with my Monopoly references and you were mine." Her sleepy voice was still infused with humor.

"You're right. If memory serves, you got to be every piece, too, didn't you? That's what you wanted."

She slid one hand behind her to trace random patterns on the bare skin of his hip. "We may have forgotten one."

"That's criminal," he murmured into her hair.

"'Go to jail and don't pass Go' is probably more appropriate."

He bent lower and kissed her bare shoulder. "Forget the $200. I look really bad in orange. We'll have to make a Monopoly date soon to rectify our mistake."

"But this is your bed. It should be the Monopoly mecca."

His cock kicked, thumping her lower back like a sledge-hammer.

"See? Your body agrees."

"Grace...you have to sleep, baby. I'll survive one—" *long, miserable, impossible, never-ending* "—night. Holding you is enough for now."

"But it's not everything you want," she whispered, sliding her hand down to brush the edge of one testicle.

He shivered hard enough to shake the little bed. "I'm trying to be as much a gentleman about this as a naked man can be."

"Seize the moment, Justin." Her hand continued to explore until she reached the root of his cock. She wrapped her hand around his base and gently squeezed.

He groaned and thrust into her grip. "Don't do that again."

She stilled. "Why not?"

"I was trying reverse psychology. For a doctor, I suck at it."

Her laughter was its own reward. When she squeezed him again, though, and began to stroke? He might as well have won the jackpot. Any jackpot.

Letting go, she wiggled and rolled over until they faced each other in the alarm clock's pale illumination. Her skin was ethereal, almost translucent in the artificial light. Her hair was spread across the pillow and she'd pulled the sheet down to her waist. She licked her lips with exacting slowness.

"You're killing me," he murmured softly, stroking her hair away from her temple and tucking it behind her ear.

"Definitely not my intent. I want you."

The admission was so quiet he was sure he must have misunderstood. "You want me."

She smiled. "Yeah. I do." Reaching up, she pulled his

face toward her and kissed him, her lips a whisper across his. "I really do."

The second kiss, firmer than the first, began to unravel him. Hell, who was he trying to kid? He'd been coming undone since she walked into his life.

Scooping her up, he rolled over on his back and settled her knees on either side of him. Her bare sex rode the ridge of his erection as he pulled her forward to claim her mouth with searing authority. In a clash of heat and sweet sounds of desire, he took her higher with that kiss. One hand roamed over every inch of bare skin he could touch while the other fisted her hair and refused to let her break the kiss to come up for air. Not that she tried. But exercising control over her did wicked things to him.

His hips surged off the bed when she ground against him, her heat like a brand. It labeled him hers, now and always.

Her soft mewl said as much as her hips did. She was hungry for him. Almost as hungry as he was for her. Almost. He just couldn't believe she could possibly want him as much as he did her, love him as much as he loved her. He'd have to bring her around to accepting his love, but that was for another time. This was about the now, just as she'd said.

Pulling her hair gently, he broke the kiss. His chest heaved. "I don't have a condom."

"I haven't ever had unprotected sex," she admitted a little shyly.

The caveman in him wanted to roar. He could be her first and last, her only, skin to skin in that hot heat of her channel. He nearly lost control right then.

Swallowing hard, he nodded. "I've been tested regularly for eight years now and I'm clean. You on the pill?"

She nodded. "No secret babies tucked away anywhere?" she asked, half teasing but clearly half serious.

"No secret babies." The image of her swollen with his child made his breath catch in his chest. He wanted to see her that way someday.

"Justin?"

"It's…" He started to say "nothing" but that would have been a lie. Instead, he let his mouth curl up on one side. "I want you, Ms. Cooper. I want you in the worst way." Refocusing, he cupped her face and leaned up to kiss her softly, quickly. "No condom?"

"No condom."

His hands rested on the slight swells of her hips. "Take what you want, Grace. If I have it to give, *anything* I have to give, it's yours."

She slipped down to his knees and, without warning, bent forward to take him in between her lips. Deep. So deep.

Justin's hips surged off the bed as he shouted. He had no idea what he said. All he knew was that one minute he was watching her and the next his eyes had rolled back in his head as he babbled words of love and affection like a virgin schoolboy. Nothing had ever felt so good. Ever. And nothing would feel like this again, this first time she loved him with her lips and teeth and tongue.

He fought the desire to watch, certain he'd lose control and embarrass himself in spectacular fashion as she took him higher and higher.

She was economy of motion and languid movement all in one.

When he couldn't take it any longer, he leaned forward and cupped one hand under her chin, pulling her up for a swift kiss. "Have to have you now. Don't want to wait. Can't wait." Caveman speak if ever he'd spoken it, but there it was. She reduced him to the most fundamental, basic forms of communication. He was one step short of grabbing her by the shoulders, flipping her over and driving into her like an animal. Fighting that age-old instinct, he forced himself to lie down again. "Take what you want, Grace."

Hesitant, moving with care, she lifted his heavy erection off his belly and straddled the wide head. Sinking slowly, her head fell back and she gasped as he breeched her outer folds. She worked herself onto him as he watched, rising and falling and taking more of him every time she lowered her lithe body.

Lost to the moment, he tore the shirt off her and placed her hands over her breasts. "Take."

She began to massage her breasts, tweaking her nipples far harder than he would have imagined was comfortable. But the tiny buds pearled quickly as she made the final thrust home. Wet heat, tight and scalding, wrapped around him, pulling him deep only to release him when she drew herself off his length. Finding her rhythm, she rode him with absolute abandon.

He slid a hand across her hip to the juncture of her thighs, parting her flesh until he found her clitoris. He flicked it with his thumb, hard.

She cried out, her rhythm faltering.

So he did it again.

What had been wanton abandon became a driving, instinctive passion as she held his hand in place and rode him harder. "Please, Justin."

Exposing the little bud, he thrummed it quickly.

That was all it took.

Justin bent his knees and Grace fell forward, her hands connecting with his chest. Gripping her hips, he pumped into her with brutal efficiency. The laws of love said he couldn't drive her higher without following, so when she came apart with a shout and her internal muscles clamped down, they pulled his orgasm out without mercy.

The burn at the base of his spine spread fast and hard.

His testicles drew up impossibly tight. He wanted to shout, but pleasure rendered him mute as he bowed off the bed, teeth gritted.

Everything he'd thought he'd known about sex and orgasms had just gone out the window. This, *this* was what it was to make love. Maybe a little rough, yes, but one thing held absolutely true. Without a doubt, he'd never experienced anything like this before.

Grace tumbled forward onto his chest, her breathing fast and labored. "Justin," she said, sleepy awe in her voice. "You held out on me Saturday night."

He held her to him, pulling the covers over them as their bodies cooled. She was already softly whuffling into his shoulder, and he listened as sleep reclaimed her.

Tucking the covers around her, he wound his arms around her and laid his lips to her temple. There was so much to say to her, so much he wanted her to know. Where to begin? He played out different scenarios over and over, discouraged when none of them seemed quite right.

Sleep claimed him before he figured it out.

16

THE NEXT DAY was a series of stops and starts. Grace spent a huge portion of it trying not to stare at Justin—and failing. She was mortified she'd come undone in front of him, but she also realized it had been a long time coming. She'd been undermined at every opportunity, underloved every chance at every turn. No one came away from something like that unscarred. That Justin had let her be today, that he didn't hound her with questions but had instead let her do her job, was critical.

But with five o'clock fast approaching, she knew she had some decisions to make. She couldn't afford a night in a hotel, and absolutely wouldn't let him pay for her. Which left his place. Not the best idea.

He caught her watching the clock when he spun his chair around and faced her. "I made a phone call earlier."

Her fingers went to ice and cold sweat popped along her nape. "What did you do?" She hated that the accusation was apparent in the question, but she was still fragile and unsure where she stood with him. What they'd shared last night had been off the charts as far as her experience went, but she didn't know if it had been the same for him.

He leaned back in his chair. "I called my apartment complex manager and made arrangements to get you a key. You can stay with me until we can get your living arrangements sorted out. Of course, you don't have to stay there. It's just an option."

She couldn't decide whether to grouse at his high-handed approach or throw herself at him with gratitude. Settling for somewhere in the middle, she nodded and offered him a small smile. "Thanks."

The tiny sound was almost lost in the space of his office. Her heart expanded until she wondered if her ribs might crack.

He'd moved her in with him. He'd taken care of everything, given her options, offered to help her get set up on her own or become a more permanent part of his life. "What if it doesn't work?"

"I'm pretty responsible, so I would imagine I can manage my own place just fine."

Again, she was forced to clarify. "No. What I meant was what if it doesn't work out between us? What if this is just some highly charged emotional save-the-damsel response you're having and you want to kick me out of your apartment in a few days?"

"I imagine we'll fight, Grace. Couples do. But it doesn't have to be ugly or violent or terminal. We're both educated psychologists. We should, in theory, be able to work through our differences."

She swiveled her chair toward her little section of the desk to garner as much privacy as she could. "Can I think about it?"

"Yeah."

His strained answer made her peek over her shoulder. The skin around his eyes had tightened even though the rest of his body appeared relaxed. That's how she knew he was lying. Well, maybe not "lying," but he sure wasn't giving her the complete truth. She'd let it ride for now. There was too much else to handle. "Where will I sleep?"

"With me if you're comfortable with that."

Grace's throat tightened. "Okay. We'll try it. One day, er, night at a time."

"Aren't you going to acknowledge the 'couples' comment?" he asked quietly.

Her mouth was so dry she could have sharecropped space right off her tongue. She had to swallow a couple of times before she answered. "You want honesty?"

"Always."

His nearly vehement response shocked her into turning around fully. "I didn't even think twice about it."

"And why is that?"

Heat burned up her neck. "It sounded natural, okay?"

He was at her side in a moment, pulling her from her chair the next. Wrapping her in his strong embrace, he spun her around while he grinned like a loon.

She laughed. "Put me down, you idiot."

"Grace Cooper is my girlfriend."

Her lips twitched. "I suppose she is."

"Lucky girl."

"Lucky *guy.*"

He kissed the tip of her nose. "No doubt." Glancing back at the clock, he sighed. "Finally five. Ready to get out of here?"

"Yeah." She reached for her messenger bag but he snatched it up before she could. "You going to carry my books, too?" she teased, hoisting up the three texts she was using to help her with the day's case notes.

Justin wiggled his fingers. "Hand 'em over."

"I might be a damsel, but I'm not in distress." She rolled her lips together, fighting the bad habit she had of chewing on them. "Not anymore, anyway."

"You were never in distress, honey. You were just stressed out. Big difference."

"Explain it to me…on the way home." She felt a small

smile tug at the corners of her mouth when he grinned widely.

"Do you mind if we move your potpie lesson up to tonight? It's the only night that works for my mom's schedule. She's very motherly, so cut her a little slack. She's going to hover and do everything but find a way to measure your emotional barometer, but it's because she cares."

"But she doesn't know me."

"Not yet, but she wants me to be happy, and you make me happy."

Grace's hand tightened on the strap of her briefcase. If she failed to make Justin happy, she'd not only lose him but the potential she had to be part of his family and an intimate in his circle of friends. Granted, she'd still have her friends, but they were all over the country.

But if she did make him happy? She could have it all. For the first time in her life, the thought of staying in Seattle didn't make her want to change her name and join the circus. She was content with the idea, so long as she was with Justin. He seemed to be the nucleus to her world at the moment. Or maybe she was the nucleus and he orbited her, bringing with him still others who would orbit them.

There was still the issue of her dreams, the promise of the opportunity in Baltimore and reuniting with Meg. None of it could come to pass if she made this a long-term choice. And she'd really only started "dating" Justin a few days ago. Should she give it all up for an uncertain future? Could she let go of the anger at her mother, a lifetime of hurt and neglect, in order to choose Seattle as her home?

Too many confusing and conflicting thoughts crowded her mind. She had to gain some perspective.

He surprised her when he took her hand.

She yanked it away. "You can't hold my hand here. You could lose your job and I could fail this practicum."

Arching a brow, he glanced down at her. "How do you

think it's going to look when you show up at the company Christmas party with me? You can only be an intern so long."

"But I have to pass this class, Justin. I can't afford for them to believe you're unduly biased."

He stopped and, again, ran his hands through his hair. "You're right. I'm just so damn proud of having you on my arm and I don't want to let anything or anyone squash that feeling, but you're right." He let go of her hand. "For what it's worth? I won't pass you just because you're phenomenal in bed. That's simply a perk."

Swatting him arm, she laughed. "You're a mess. Ever considered getting your head checked out?"

"Been there, done that. That's how I ended up becoming a psychologist, why it was so important to me to get my doctorate and come work here. The psychologist I saw at Second Chances convinced me I was smart enough, empathetic enough and decidedly bullheaded enough to make the ideal doctoral student."

"I wondered," she admitted. "I went straight through to get my master's so I would be sure to get a job that would enable me to pay my own way in life. I guess I also wanted to figure my mom out, why she treated me the way she does. Did. The way she did. I'm done with her now."

"Good." He stroked a hand down the back of her head as they walked down the hall, dropping it the moment she gave him a hard look. "I don't want you going to her, or her house, for anything. We'll get you new clothes, though underwear are optional," he whispered, waggling his brows.

"Dirty old man," she whispered in response.

"Every chance I get." He slowed his pace until they were facing each other on the sidewalk outside. "For as long as you'll let me."

She surprised herself by having an immediate answer at the ready.

"Settle in for the long haul."

JUSTIN WASHED HIS HANDS in the sink in his mom's kitchen. They had to have their lesson here because he didn't have pots and pans. Yet. He would, but everything would have to come together slowly. Maybe Grace could pick out a few things for the apartment, things that would help her put her stamp on the place and make it more their home instead of his.

Drying his hands, he bit the inside of his cheek and tried not to smile. *Home.* There, with him. It didn't get better than that.

Grace turned, her cheeks rosy from the heat of the stove, her eyes no longer shadowed but bright. He wanted to see her like this every day for the rest of their lives.

"What?" she asked.

Leaning a hip against the counter, he crossed his arms over his chest and shook his head. If he kept this up, these emotional revelations paired with images of happily-ever-after, he supposed he'd have the wedding invites in the mail before he even proposed.

Darcy said something to Grace before shifting to another task at the counter. Grace met Justin's gaze. "I love her," she mouthed.

Justin grinned. All these silent conversations and dancing around as he and Grace tried to be on their best behavior. To hell with that.

Closing the distance between them, Justin picked Grace up and kissed her, fast and sure. "You're absolutely delicious covered in pastry."

"Your shirt's going to have to be treated to get the Crisco out. Sorry."

"No worries. Our place has a washer and dryer."

Darcy's brows rose but she didn't say anything.

"Did I forget to mention I'm dragging Grace along and subjecting her to the sheer torture of living with me as my live-in love slave?" he asked his mother innocently.

Grace's face flamed red, but Darcy just laughed, swatting him. "Cut it out, Justin Alexander. You're embarrassing both of us, and for what?"

"The pretty blushes that stain my girls' faces."

"Your flattery will get you nowhere with me." Darcy took an onion out of the small wooden keeper next to the canisters and tossed it to him. "You two finish up in here while I go round up your sisters and make sure their homework is done. We'll eat as soon as you call us down."

As soon as his mother left, Justin let his girlfriend slide down his front and did his level best to ignore the way she molded against him, her curves, strength and soft spots each a temptation. It wouldn't kill him to keep his hands to himself. For now, anyway. Tonight? She was all his.

Two hours later, the house smelled like heaven. Justin emerged from the small downstairs bathroom and stopped just short of the kitchen doorway. The two women were sitting at the table sipping, presumably, cups of tea and sharing some private time. He wanted to know what they were talking about, but he also didn't want to interrupt. Conflicted, he stood there longer than he should have.

"Come in, honey. We can hear you lurking out there."

He closed his eyes and shook his head. "Not lurking, Mom. Just trying to figure out how to grab a Coke from the fridge without interrupting."

"Don't tell me that, of all your mad skills, you're not a certified ninja, too," Grace said with mock disgust.

"I'll make it a bullet point on my five-year plan. 'Become a certified ninja.'" He walked into the kitchen and went straight for the fridge to grab his soda. The oven timer pinged.

"Grab that while you're there?" Darcy asked. She sighed, propping her chin in her hand. "Seems it was only yesterday I was cooking this very meal just to make sure you came home at night."

Justin nearly dropped the pie plate when Grace asked, "Where would he have been that he would have possibly missed this?"

Silence hung in the room and thickened the atmosphere.

Grace set her teacup down, her brows drawing together. "Justin?"

"You'll excuse me for a moment." Darcy pushed away from the table and hurried from the kitchen.

This wasn't remotely close to how he'd envisioned having this conversation, but he couldn't avoid it any longer. Unbuttoning his shirt, he shrugged out of the left sleeve. The elaborate tattoo that banded his biceps felt tighter than a manacle. *Illusion*, he thought. It had been the same way the first three or four years after he'd cut himself off from Deuce-8.

"This?" He traced a finger along the outside center of the design.

"I've seen it."

"Right." He took a generous sip of his soda before setting the can back down and spinning it slowly around in the ring of condensation. "I..." He cleared his throat and forced himself to meet her steady gaze. "Grace, I was in Deuce-8 for almost five years." The way the blood left her face made him rush to explain. "Three weeks shy of my sixteenth birthday, a guy offered me a hundred bucks to deliver a note to someone a few blocks away. That's how it started. Small stuff."

"Why?" The quiet question held no judgment but a world of confusion.

"My dad was killed in military service and we were desperate for money. I'd take the money and slip an extra five or ten into my mom's wallet, put gas in the car, buy groceries and sneak them into the house. I thought it bought protection for my family." He tunneled his fingers through his hair, pulling until it hurt. "I got in way over my head, but I got out. I've been free from that lifestyle for a little over a decade. The minute I got my first legit paycheck, I had my rank covered up." He took her hand and traced her fingers over his ink. "I wanted a clean break. I *needed* it. I'd never have made it to twenty-one if I hadn't gotten out when I did."

She followed the intricate design around his biceps. "What did you do for them?"

"I started as a courier and ended as an enforcer."

"Did you ever kill anyone?"

Closing his eyes, he fought to center his emotions and control the moment that threatened to overwhelm him. "I did. Yes." He risked a glance at her.

Her face had blanched. She tried to pick her teacup up but her hands shook so badly she only spilled the tepid contents all over the table. "I-I'm sorry."

"It was an ugly, ugly life. Second Chances saved me when I was too stupid to save myself. I was in and out of jail several times before I landed on their doorstep as a final chance to straighten up. I owe them so much. It's why it's so important for me to work there." He swallowed hard enough he nearly choked. "I want to give back to the program that saved me, and I want to give other kids the same opportunity."

"Why did they let you go?"

"Deuce?"

She nodded furiously.

"I fought my way out. Literally. Think cage fighting but with weapons. It was ugly."

"It nearly killed him," Darcy said from the doorway. "But he made it." She moved in and laid a hand on Justin's shoulder. "Don't hold the past against him."

"I can't change who I was, Grace. Therapy taught me that much. The most I can do is try my damnedest to be a better person. I had to forgive myself for being responsible for a lot of ugliness. You have every right to know who I once was, but I want you to see me for who I am now."

And that was the crux of the entire evolutionary cycle he'd been caught up in. It came down to now, to this very moment, when he was either rejected or absolved.

Grace turned huge green eyes to him and stared, seeming to gaze straight through him to his most intimate parts.

He let her look, silently pleading with her to glimpse the man he wanted to be for her.

17

GRACE COULD ONLY stare at Justin with a combination of horror and admiration. Horror that he'd been such a violent young man; admiration that he'd clawed his way out of the lifestyle and turned himself around. It all made sense now. "That's why you let me take the lead with Gavin. You knew it would be more effective."

Justin reached for her hand, stopping when she involuntarily flinched. "I understood how to handle him because it was how I was handled. The rest? You did it on your own—the comic-book connection, the firm but compassionate female authority figure, the camaraderie. But I also realized I was also too close to be entirely objective. I've got to get over that if I'm going to make this work at the program."

"You'll deal with a lot of kids involved in various gangs." The thought made her want to vomit. How could she be involved with a man who would put himself in constant danger daily just by showing up to work? Who would willingly dive into the kind of malignant environment she was so desperately trying to leave behind? She wasn't sure it was something she could live with.

"I will, yes. But hopefully I'll be a positive influence on them and help them realize they've got options." He closed the distance between their hands and laced their fingers together. "Please, Grace. Trust who you know I am now, not who I used to be."

"You killed people."

"I did. I'll never be proud of it, but it was a 'me or them' situation each time."

"How many times?" When he hesitated, her fingers spasmed in his grasp. "How many times, Justin?"

"Less than ten."

She shuddered. *Any one of those instances could have gone a different direction.* "You should have turned yourself into the police."

His hand spasmed. "Probably, but I never did. Do you want me to?"

"No." The answer erupted from her. "No," she repeated, quieter.

"I have to move forward. If I stay still and look back…" He dragged his free hand down his face.

"The nightmares can be brutal, even now," Darcy interjected. "Justin, would you give me a moment with Grace? You can go let your sisters know that dinner's on in five minutes and they should wash up."

He silently rose and left the room.

The moment his heavy footsteps sounded on the stairs, Darcy faced her. "Be careful with him." The plea was little more than a breath. "He was in such a bad place after he lost his father. Caught up in my own grief, I wasn't enough for him. He suffered for it. I don't want to see him suffer again." She took a deep breath and looked up, eyes as blue as her son's. "When he loves, he does it wholeheartedly. And that means he takes loss harder than most. I don't want him to go through that kind of loss again."

Grace answered honestly. "First, everyone processes grief differently. You never stopped loving Justin, and I'm sure he got that beyond a shadow of a doubt. He had to find his way out of his own grief. You were waiting for him when he did. That's love and, I'd be willing to wager, that's also where he learned about how to love." *Love.* Justin hadn't said anything about love. He cared for her, yes. But love? "Second, I'm not at all sure that he loves me, Darcy."

The other woman smiled softly then, her face appearing an easy decade younger without the worry. "He's my baby boy, my first child. *I* learned what love really was when I had him. Trust me when I tell you I can recognize it at ten paces on a moonless night." She took Grace's hands. "Are you in love, sweetie? How do you feel about him?"

Grace's pulse sped up and her heart hammered when she thought of Justin, being in Justin's arms, hearing Justin's laugh, basking in his compassionate warmth, smelling his cologne, seeing those blue eyes lock on hers in moments of absolute passion. Goose bumps spread up her arms and she shivered.

"That says plenty," Darcy murmured.

"A physical reaction is one thing, but…I'm not sure. It's impossible to be sure that what I'm experiencing is that be-all and end-all that I want." She dropped her gaze. "That sounds very childish, doesn't it?"

Darcy hooked a work-worn finger under Grace's chin and gently lifted her head until their eyes met. "That's not childish at all, Grace. Those are the words of a woman who won't settle for less than being the reason a man draws his every breath."

Grace swallowed around the lump in her throat, searching Darcy's face, taking comfort in the compassion and wisdom that rested there. The older woman was right. Grace wouldn't settle for less. She'd witnessed firsthand years of casual sex and meaningless relationships erode her mother's willingness to invest in another human being. Relationships of any type were too much work, and Cindy didn't work.

No, she'd chosen to let Grace long for love as a child, abused her for wanting love as a young teen and berated her as a young adult for being foolish enough to hunger for it. Now? The final break had come because Cindy had tried to taint Grace's conviction that she could find a man who made her believe love was possible. That was the real crux of the matter. Deep down, Grace wanted Justin to love her. She wanted to be the moon to his sun, the fuel to his flame…the reason he drew his every breath. She wanted him to prove she was lovable when all she'd ever heard was the opposite. That Cindy intended to steal that from her? No. That was the line in the sand no one crossed. It was time to drop her mother's emotional baggage and move on, to make a clean break and be free from the nightmares altogether. She was done with Cindy. That meant she was free to go where she wanted to go and be who she wanted to be.

"Grace?"

Justin's voice pulled her from her emotional tailspin before she crashed and burned.

She rose from her chair and moved to him, peripherally aware that Darcy had stepped out of the kitchen. Lacing her hands together behind Justin's neck, she pulled him toward her, silently thrilled when his hands went to her waist and his lips found hers. The kiss was nearly reverent, a declaration of unspoken desire between them. It told of hopes and dreams for the future, wishes waiting to be fulfilled. It reassured her that she was precious and cherished and wanted, that she had a place with this man. It said almost everything Grace wanted it to say but, when she broke away to meet his deep blue eyes, the one thing she most needed she didn't get. He didn't tell her he loved her.

That was fine. She would wait.

Holding his gaze, she chose her words carefully. "That

conversation is closed. I see who you are. What you were? That's past. Just promise me you'll keep it there."

His brows drew together. "I would never let that violence come near you."

She rubbed her thumb over his stubbled chin. "I'll hold you to that."

They set the table, moving around each other like satellites orbiting a planet, passing close but never touching. There was so much she wanted to say, yet years of rejection rendered her mute. She had no doubt she was going to have to ditch the insecurities and claim what she wanted if she intended to influence the outcome.

Turning to Justin, she found him watching her with the strangest expression. "What?" she asked.

"Nothing." With a small shrug, he grabbed pot holders and set the chicken potpie in the center of the table at the same time more than one pair of feet clattered down the stairs.

"Melody has a friend over." He leaned across the table. "Unfortunately it's—" He smiled over her shoulder. "Hi, Jenny."

If she hadn't known him as well as she already did, hadn't watched him deal with women at the club, she never would have picked up on his discomfort. She glanced over his shoulder and found Melody rolling her eyes as a young girl, probably fifteen or sixteen, gazed at Justin with open longing. Grace felt for Jenny. She understood how miserable it was to love someone and not have them love you in return. She decided to help the girl out.

Jenny noticed Grace and looked at her with confusion just as Justin moved to Grace's side. Grace recognized the exact minute—when Justin's hand landed on her waist—that Jenny realized Grace was Justin's girlfriend. Her eyes widened and her mouth fell open.

Grace stepped forward. "Hi, Jenny. Justin's told me a lot about you."

The girl considered her for the briefest second before glancing at Justin. "He has?"

Grace offered her hand. Jenny shook it, still staring fixedly at Justin. "He has. Apparently you're a pretty regular fixture at the Maxwell house." Smiling, Grace retrieved the hand Jenny kept shaking. "Justin was teaching me how to make chicken potpie."

"You can't cook?" the girl asked, obviously aiming for disdain.

"Nope. Not unless you count opening cans of soup. I make a mean can of soup."

"I've taken home economics. I can make a bunch of stuff," Jenny said assertively.

"That's cool." Grace sat in the seat Justin pulled out for her. "What's your best dish?"

Jenny eyed her suspiciously. "I make really awesome lasagna."

"I love lasagna! Would you teach me how to make it? Here? I'm sure Justin wouldn't mind helping us cut up ingredients. He helped out tonight."

Jenny was so obviously thrown for a loop, Grace wondered if she'd done more harm than good. The girl was unsure whether to like Grace or hate her for being with Justin. Instead of pushing, Grace let her work through it. Before she could speak, Melody started to answer.

Grace shook her head. "It's Jenny's best meal so she should be the one to teach me this time, okay?"

Melody sighed. "Whatevs."

Jenny finally nodded slowly. "If Justin will help cut stuff up."

"He will." Grace eyed him levelly. "Won't you?"

"Sure." He smiled.

Darcy hustled in. "Hi, Jenny. I'm glad you stayed for dinner."

"Justin's here, Mom. Of course she stayed."

"Melody Ann, mind your manners."

The bite in Darcy's words made the teen dip her chin. "I apologize."

"You owe the apology to Jenny, not me."

"Sorry, Jen. It just freaks me out that you totally think Justin's hot."

Jenny blushed furiously.

"As far as apologies go, that may have been the most awkward thing I've ever heard. Regardless," Justin drawled, winking at Jenny, "I have an affinity for any woman who appreciates the fact I'm hot. Thank you."

Grace's heart, which had been already full to overflowing, swelled even more. Justin was so kind, even as uncomfortable as he was. He continued to prove over and over what an amazing man he was, and Grace realized her comments about Prince Charming hadn't been so far off the mark. He was everything a woman could want, and here he was. Asking to be hers.

"Moon eyes?" Justin leaned over and whispered, lips twitching against her ear. "Not you, too."

She laughed, couldn't help it. "Yeah. Sorry."

"Don't apologize for making me a lucky man." Grace looked down at her plate, fighting to regain her equilibrium as Justin reached for the pie server. "Okay. Who's up first?"

THE NEXT COUPLE of days passed without incident for Justin. Until Friday. Gavin, the kid being courted by Deuce-8, skipped his third counseling appointment. Justin called his parole officer to report the skip only to be told by the harried woman that he'd also skipped school both Thursday and Friday. No one seemed to know where he was, family included.

Nausea hit Justin hard enough he grabbed the trash can and fought not to retch. He couldn't lose the kid to the gang. Justin wanted to save the kid from a lifetime of violence and regret, a lifetime that would, in all likelihood, kill him before he was even old enough to vote. He'd been there. He knew. He also knew there was a solid chance the gang had upped their pressure to pull the kid deeper, to separate him from his regular life. They'd make him believe he was important, irreplaceable, wanted. They'd give him cash, drugs, women—whatever it took to get him to commit. Then they'd use him like the pawn he was, another body in the ever-growing turf war.

An image of the kid, eyes open but blinded by death, rose in his mind. Bile rushed up his throat. Too far lost to memories and emotions, he couldn't stop himself from vomiting.

Grace entered as he set the trash can down. She took in everything—the phone pulled close, his pallor, the reek of bile—and shut the door very quietly. "What happened?"

He pulled his tie off and wiped his mouth. "Gavin's missing."

"No." Her hushed refusal to accept the truth made the muscles along her shoulder tighten more. "I'd wanted to believe he was just late today."

Glancing at the clock, he shook his head. "'Late' is fifteen minutes, not three hours."

"I didn't want to give up hope," she said, low and hard. "Sometimes it's all a person's got."

The only thing he could do was nod and accept the bottle of soda she slid his way. Rinsing his mouth, he stood. "I've got to update the director so we can increase security."

"Why?"

Stopping at the door, he looked back, his stare blank. "If Gavin admitted to Deuce's leaders that he talked to us, they might retaliate against us for screwing with their recruit."

"I hate that you're so familiar with this."

The heartache in her words wrecked him. He'd disappointed so many people over his thirty years, letting them down with varying degrees of failure. He didn't want to pull a repeat performance with her. Never with her. "Forgive the bile breath."

Her brows drew together. "Huh?"

Stepping up to her, he drew her into a fierce hug and laid his cheek on the top of her head. His heart rate slowed and his stomach settled some when she wrapped her arms around his waist in return. "Thank you."

"For what?" she asked.

"This." He stayed that way longer than he should have, but he couldn't seem to let go. It slowly dawned on him that she was as much a safe haven for him as he was for her. In a different way, maybe, but still a place of refuge all the same.

He breathed her in, the smell of her shampoo combining with her warm skin to form a heady smell. Her hair, down today, hung over his arms in loose waves. The way her body molded to his—or maybe his molded to hers?—was as close to perfection as nature could get. Sleeping with her the past few nights, no sex but true sleep, and waking up to her every morning had cemented the fact he loved her. He'd never wanted another woman like this, long-term.

Forever.

She looked up at him, rubbing her temple. "You okay?"

"Sorry about that. I'm fine." The intercom beeped. "Grace?"

She stepped out of his embrace. "Yes?"

"There's a delivery for you at the front desk."

"What is it?"

The receptionist chuckled. "An amazing bouquet of roses."

Grace glanced at Justin, brows raised.

His heart plummeted. He hadn't sent her flowers.

The door handle rattled.

He shoved Grace aside as the door opened and he was suddenly staring down the barrel of a gun.

18

"STAY THERE, GRACE. Do *not* turn around."

Those were the first words that registered with Grace. "Excuse me?" she snapped, irritated. What the hell had he shoved her for? Did he think the door was going to hit her harder than he had when it opened? It had been locked, for heaven's sake. She made to stand.

"Damn it, Grace," Justin snapped. "Stay. Down."

She cradled her hands, scraped raw on the industrial carpet. She glanced over her shoulder as Gavin stepped inside the office brandishing a 9 mm Berretta. A *cocked* 9 mm Berretta. "Oh, shit," she breathed.

Gavin shut the door and locked it, refusing to look down at her. "You aren't supposed to be here, Grace." Gone was the "Ms." he usually addressed her with. She started to roll over and his trigger finger shifted from running down the side of the barrel to hovering over the trigger, the gun still pointed at Justin. "Uh-uh. You stay there and do what Maxwell says. Turn around."

She stopped moving, her heart wedged so tightly in her shrunken throat she couldn't breathe. "Don't do this," she quietly pleaded. She wasn't trying to exert her influence as an authority figure. She was expressing the truth of her vulnerability. Gone were all the reasons to talk this out with him professionally. Gone were all the lessons she'd ever learned by living in a domestic war zone. Gone were her years of training. All that remained was a woman facing the prospect of losing the man she loved when she'd only just found him. "Please, Gavin." Her voice broke on his name.

"Stay down, Grace," the teen commanded. "I don't want you exposed to this kind of violence."

Laughter colored with madness escaped her in a whoosh. "You don't, huh?" She rolled to her side, refusing to look away, afraid of what could happen in that blink of an eye. Fear threatened to shut her mind down. Then she gazed up at Justin. He was facing the young man, hands loose at his sides, face completely neutral. She owed it to him, to them, to what might be, to do better than freeze. As if on cue, her mind began to work. *Use his name.* "You're the one exposing me to the violence, Gavin."

She rolled a little farther, and his finger shifted to rest on the trigger. "I told you, stay down."

"Please, Gavin. Don't do this." *Make it personal.* "Don't do this to me."

"I ain't doing nothing to *you*, Grace. I'm taking out a traitor to D'eight," he spat, using the gang's common name. "You know this dude is a traitor, right?"

Keep his focus on you. "Wait. What do you mean he's a traitor?"

Gavin spat on Justin's shoes. "He was full Deuce. The brothers had his back. They were gonna provide for his momma and her kids. All he had to do was cap a cop who'd worked his way into Deuce. Woulda been easy, but he broke faith, Grace. He wouldn't pull the trigger."

"The guy had a family," Justin said softly. "A wife, small kids, his own mother living with him."

"Shut up!" Gavin shouted, hand shaking so hard Grace was terrified he was going to accidentally shoot Justin. "You shut up."

Justin shrugged, and Grace jumped in before he could say anything else. "What do you get out of this, Gavin? What does—" she almost lost it "—killing Justin get you?"

"I'll be full Deuce. The boys'll bring me in, take care of *my* family like they woulda his."

"They're lying to you," Justin said calmly.

Gavin raised the gun to Justin's face. "Shut. Up."

Grace began to sweat, her muscles aching from sustaining the same position too long. "Gavin, please. Don't do this to me. And you *are* the one doing this."

"I'm gonna make you rich, Grace."

"Rich?" she asked, confusion making her shake her head quickly.

"D'eight's going to pay me hard for taking out this muthuh. When I'm rich, I'll come for you, take care of you in style."

"You can't believe I'm going to go with you if you shoot Justin?" No way could she say "kill" again. Once was one time too many. Everyone had limits. That was hers.

"He'll take you, by force if has to," Justin said, still calm.

The teen shoved the nose of the handgun into the soft spot under Justin's chin. "I ain't tellin' you again to shut your fuckin' mouth, Pretty Boy."

Grabbing the detail, she asked, "Why'd you call him Pretty Boy?"

"It was the name D'eight gave him. I'm Code 3," he said with pride.

"Why Code 3?" she pressed. *Get him to talk about himself.*

"Because I'm going to be their point man." When she didn't comment, he smiled affectionately. "Means I'll be head of the enforcers' unit. You'll learn."

"You're going to ruin my life, Gavin." She looked up at

him, forcing herself to focus on his face and not the gun or Justin. *Keep face-to-face contact.*

"I'm going to *make* your life, Grace. You're going to love me," he said, cocking his head to the side in an attempt at being coy.

"I'm never going to be able to trust you." *Get to the root of the issue.*

"Like you can trust this turncoat?" he scoffed, the first vestiges of insecurity showing through his facade as he glanced between her and Justin.

"I do trust him. Completely."

Gavin blinked quickly. "How can you? How can you trust someone who didn't stand by what they said they'd do?"

Clarify emotions. "I feel about him the way you want me to feel about you."

"Tell me," Justin said softly.

This wasn't the way it was supposed to happen. There should have been time, a hundred thousand hours to say this a hundred thousand different ways, but now she was reduced to the most basic truth, offering the only answer she could. "I love you, Justin Maxwell. I've loved you for years." She faced Gavin. "If you shoot him? I will never, ever forgive you. You want my respect? You want me to believe you're an honorable man?" She finished rolling over and sat up, palms out. "Do the right thing here. We can all walk away from this."

"I can't," Gavin whispered, the gun lowering a fraction. "I have to—"

Justin lunged, grabbing the barrel of the gun. He grabbed the barrel of the gun, shoving it up and back, twisting to break Gavin's hold on the weapon between heartbeats. The kid didn't have the opportunity to squeeze off a shot before Justin had control of the gun and had aimed it at his attacker.

Grace scrambled off the floor and reached for the phone. "Don't."

The absolute vacancy of emotion in Justin's voice stopped her cold. "What?"

"On your knees, Gavin. Hands behind your head."

The kid paled so hard and fast Grace feared he might pass out, but he did what Justin demanded. A dark stain appeared on his jeans where he wet himself.

Justin didn't react. "I'm going to make a few things crystal clear for you before we finish this. First, don't ever, *ever* think you can bring violence against Grace and not face repercussions. I will defend her to my last breath.

"Second? They call you Code because that's how they expect you to arrive at the emergency room. Dead, you dumbass. Coded. As in, no medical assistance required because this piece of shit is beyond help. And you're number three because there are two other Codes in front of you. You guys are just collateral. They don't give a damn whether you live or die. I was in Deuce for years. Years, Gavin. You think they really believed you'd take me down? I've done the kind of stuff you haven't even begun to *dream of*, kid."

"Nuh-uh," Gavin said weakly.

"Believe what you want. Third? The only reason this hasn't ended differently is because I won't bring the violence to Grace. Not like you did. She deserves a life free of the mess you wanted to subject her to. You would sentence her to death out of some misbegotten sense of entitlement to her?"

Grace watched Justin struggle with something she didn't completely understand. Watched as his hands shook and his pupils dilated. "Justin?" she said again.

He kept on as if he hadn't heard her. "You think I'm going to just up and let you walk out of here? You're wrong. They called me Pretty Boy because no one who looked at me believed I'd ever be able to pull the trigger, to do the dark shit that tainted the soul. I did, Gavin. More than once." His chest heaved. "If it hadn't been for the compassion of the cop I was sent to kill, I *would have done it again.* He helped me get out. So I'm going to give you a choice. You get out now and go legit, get into Second Chances and become a mentor, or your mother gets a call from the coroner this afternoon to come identify your body. Because here's what you *don't* get. No one threatens me and mine."

"You're sayin'…they sent me in here to fail?"

"Probably. You were a message to remind me to keep my nose out of their business. You were also a tool they could afford to lose. On the off chance you got the drop? They'd have owned you, man, because once you pull the trigger? The options to get out alive are pretty much nil."

Gavin folded in on himself. "But I got to take care of my mom. She lost her job, my old man's a drunk. I got a little brother."

"Then get a damn *job*, Gavin! Don't take to killing people to supply your old man with drink. Your mom deserves better than going to her son's funeral in the next three months."

"I don't got skills."

His tone softened. "If you get involved here, you can learn some. In the meantime, I happen to know a construction crew who's always looking for cleanup people. Means walking around picking up nails and boards and stuff, but it pays pretty well. I'm willing to make the call if you'll pull your head out of your ass and man up."

Grace watched as Justin retreated from the violence that had nearly claimed him. He was working this kid like a pro, scaring him, then offering him redemption and a way to save face. *Making it personal.*

She took a step toward him but he held his hand out.

"Not yet. Not while I have a gun in my hands." He stepped back, the weapon tucked up close to his body so Gavin wouldn't be able to return the favor and take it away from him. "Now what's it going to be?"

"You going to call the cops?"

"Them or the bodymobile. Your choice. You have to accept responsibility for your actions, Gavin. You chose every single move you made over the past, what, three months?"

"Two."

"Two months, then. That's what being a real man is all about—earning your way in the world, owning your mistakes and working to be a better man. It has nothing to do with what you can take by force. Feeding on those weaker than you doesn't make you better, it just makes you a target for more people—those who are stronger and want to prove a point and those who are weaker who you've done wrong." Justin clicked the gun's safety on. "Be glad I stopped subscribing to that warped take-by-force mentality a long time ago. Now, what's it going to be?"

"Call the cops."

"Make the call, Grace."

She rushed to the phone and dialed with shaking hands. When all was said and done, she turned back to Justin, fighting to keep calm.

He looked over to her and smiled even as worry continued to fill his gaze. "So, you love me, huh?"

"Enough that I'm going to absolutely kill you when this is over and we're alone again."

"She's crazy about me," he said to Gavin.

"No need to rub it in, asshole," Gavin muttered.

Justin snorted. "Yeah. There is."

"Both of you cut it out." She sank to the floor, buried her face in her hands and, through the tears, tried to make her mind slow down and work even a little logically. Everything Justin had been through had brought him here, to this moment. It had enabled him to handle staring down the barrel of a large-bore handgun without blinking, without folding, without fear. She'd grown up rough, but she was nowhere near as prepared as he'd been to embrace the violence and meet it blow for blow. What he'd done, who he'd been and who he was now, they'd all come together in those terrorizing minutes. This world was where he was meant to be—the same hell she'd worked so hard to escape. If she stayed with him, would he only pull her down again? Or would he able to show her how to do what he'd done, to find true healing in the heart of despair?

Grace looked up to find Justin watching her. "You were so comfortable with the ugliness."

He didn't answer, only stared.

Tears traced down her cheeks, hot against her chilled skin. "I don't know if I can live with that."

JUSTIN'S WORLD TILTED, throwing him off balance enough he was forced to take a step to recover, planting his feet wide. "What are you saying?"

"I'm not sure." The words were hushed but undeniably broken.

The police barged in, bringing with them a flurry of activity. They dragged Justin away from Grace as he was temporarily cuffed and the weapon taken and disarmed. By the time they hauled Gavin away, Justin was standing clear of the general ruckus and watching as the police took Grace's statement. In an absolute twist of irony, the cop he'd been sent to kill had made detective and shown up today as part of the response team the patrol unit called in after arriving.

"How's my favorite hit man doing?" Detective Stevenson asked, eyeing Justin.

"Just earned my doctorate and came back to work for

the center." It felt damn good to be able to answer him that way.

Stevenson whistled long and low. "Doctorate, huh? And you're working here?"

"It was that or join hostage negotiations for the cops, and I didn't think they'd take my application too seriously given our history."

The other man laughed. "Yeah, they'd have eighty-sixed it."

"Not surprised." Justin looked around Stevenson again, checking on Grace.

"She yours?" the detective asked, pulling out a stick of gum and offering one to Justin.

He declined. His mouth was so dry he wouldn't have been able to work up the spit to chew. "She was before this whole thing went down."

"What changed?"

"I…um. I might have lost my temper a little bit. I got it under control, but not before I scared the kid. And her."

The detective touched the side of his crooked nose. "At least you didn't break the punk's nose. Never did get this fixed. It's a solid reminder that there are always people out there who'll do you first chance they get."

Justin's stomach soured. "I'm so sorry about that."

"No, no. I'm glad it was you."

"What? Why?" Justin asked, confused. "You'll have to bear with me. I've never had anyone thank me for almost killing them before."

"Because anyone else would have pulled the trigger," the older man said softly. "You? You might have beat the crap out of me, but you were willing to listen."

"You wouldn't shut up."

"Yeah, well, you're welcome."

"Thank you." Justin peered around Stevenson to see Grace again, happy to find that Stevenson's partner, a woman, had finished taking her statement. Grace sat there nursing a cup of hot tea, eyes on the floor. "If you'll excuse me, sir. I have to make this right."

"My advice? Don't stop talking."

"Funny guy," Justin murmured.

Crossing the break room took forever. Justin felt as if he was swimming through Jell-O. The haunted look in her eyes wrecked him in a million ways, large and small. "Hey."

She nodded in answer.

"You okay?"

Another nod.

"Was the detective too rough? I can say something if she was."

This time a shake of the head.

Fear that he'd lost her climbed his spine with what must have been a pickax and climbing cleats, starting at his tailbone and scaling one vertebra for every nonanswer he received. "You have to talk to me."

She stared at him.

"Grace, please. I know what you saw in there had to be terrifying. It terrified *me*. I was so scared he'd pull the trigger before I could take the gun away, but then you started to talk to him. You defied us both and wouldn't turn around, wouldn't stop pushing. You probably saved my life." He unbuttoned the top two buttons of his shirt and whipped his chin to the side, popping his neck. "Hell, I'm certain you saved my life. And then, when you insisted on rolling over? I thought I was going to totally lose my mind. All that went through my mind was that I had to stop Gavin. I couldn't leave you, couldn't risk that being your last memory of me. But when I got the gun, I sort of, um, lost my temper." He waited, but she just stared at him. "That was exactly the way I never wanted you to see me. I'm so sorry."

"Sorry?" she croaked.

Shit. Shit, shit, shit. She was going to call it quits. It registered it in the distance that grew between them, in the absolute way he was floundering to find his footing with her. No way could he let her go. "You said you love me," he answered, voice gruff. "Don't give up on me, Grace."

"Give up." She leaned forward.

He grabbed her shoulders and pulled her up to stand. "Damn it, talk to me! Please. I'm not above getting down on my knees, begging in front of all these people."

She closed her eyes. "Don't."

"Look at me."

She shook her head.

"Look at me, Grace." He rand his hands down her arms, gripping her fingers. "Please." Slowly, so slowly he was sure he'd lose his mind, she lifted her face to his. "What do you want from me?" he asked fervently. "How do I fix this?"

"That's just the point. You can't fix it. You shouldn't. You wanted me to see you for who you are. I have now. You're meant to do this, here, but I've worked so hard to leave this very thing behind. You would have to promise me you wouldn't bring it home, but that would be a lie. You can't make that promise. "

His heart ached. "No, I can't. I can't control what might happen, can't predict what madness from my past might resurface." He cupped her face, resting his forehead against hers. "What I can promise you is this. Breakfast in bed every Sunday morning. Season tickets to the Seahawks. Friendship. No dirty underwear on the floor. Shared household chores." He kissed her nose. "A house someday. A puppy."

"You're bribing me with a puppy?"

"If it worked, I'd bribe you with a damn three-ring circus," he said fervently.

"Why?"

"Because this is where you belong, too. I may understand people's ugliness, but you bring them hope. Just look at what you've accomplished. You're free."

She closed her eyes and a short, harsh sob escaped her. She stepped out of his embrace, then around him, and headed for the door.

That's what did it. He'd always look back on it and blame that very moment, the moment he thought he'd lost her. "Marry me, Grace Cooper," he shouted across the filled room.

To a voice, everyone fell silent.

Grace stopped, her shoulders bowed and shaking, her sobs muffled behind her hand.

"Marry me," he repeated, walking toward her.

"Why?" she turned slowly. "Because of all the reasons you listed? You missed the biggest one."

He searched her face, his heart pounding. "Because I love you," he said softly. "Marry me because I love you."

Her direct stare made his gut cramp.

One eye narrowed before she asked, "Enough to get me the three-ring circus?"

"I'm not shoveling elephant crap."

A hard sob ripped through her. "You have to be who you are."

"We'll deal with things one day at a time. Together." He held out a hand, dropping it to his side when she shook her head and stepped back. "Don't do this."

"Baltimore—"

"If it's where you need to be, I'll go with you." He took a step toward her. "Marry me because I'm not the man I was and I'm only half the man I might be without you. Marry me because the thought of living without you makes me sick. Marry me because I'll love you to my last breath, whenever that happens to be. Forgive me for who I've been and focus on who I am." He closed the gap between them with another step. "Marry me, Grace. Marry me because I've loved you for so long. I won't ever intentionally bring violence to our doorstep, and I won't let my history bleed into our future. I'm not that man anymore, but I will always protect what's mine." And that, he realized, was the truth he'd been seeking from himself all along. "I'm not that man anymore," he repeated gently.

"You're right. You're not that man anymore. And I'm not the girl I was. I don't have to leave to escape. Loving you is what set me free."

Reaching out, he pinched a lock of her hair between his thumb and forefinger, rubbing gently. "You're killing me, Smalls."

She hiccuped and laughed then threw herself at him. "Yes."

He wrapped her in a fierce embrace, burying his face in her hair. "I love you so much."

"I love you, too. Don't you ever do this to me again. Ever." She hiccuped harder. "I'm going to get a job nearby so I can crisis negotiate your ass out of a sling if someone comes to kill you again. You need to be here, need to give your experiences to these kids, and I need to be with you."

His heart slammed into chest in a rapid-fire rhythm. "You'll stay."

"My heart is where you are, so yeah. Besides, I may have to go back to school after the university finds out about us."

"I spoke to the director while they were taking your statement. After today's blowup, he doesn't think we can sweep the ethics violation under the rug. I've accepted a short suspension, and he believes that'll satisfy the university. I might have to pick up a couple of extra shifts at the club, but you'll graduate."

"Thank you," she said, but she wouldn't meet his eyes.

"Look at me, Grace." He curled a finger under her chin and lifted. "I can't stop life from happening. What I can do, though, is make you this promise. Every breath I take, every beat of my heart, from now until the end, will be for you."

She smiled. "Prince Charming's got nothing on you."

"Hell, no." He leaned down and kissed her, owning her just as much as he was owned by her. "Never forget it."

"Give me a lifetime to remember and you've got yourself a deal."

He lowered his mouth to hers. "When does our lifetime officially start?"

The cheers of those around them almost drowned out her response.

"It starts now."

* * * * *

The spotlight is on Levi next!
Don't miss PULLED UNDER,
available March 2015.

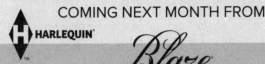

REQUEST YOUR FREE BOOKS!
2 FREE NOVELS PLUS 2 FREE GIFTS!

HARLEQUIN®
Blaze®
red-hot reads!

YES! Please send me 2 FREE Harlequin® Blaze™ novels and my 2 FREE gifts (gifts are worth about $10). After receiving them, if I don't wish to receive any more books, I can return the shipping statement marked "cancel." If I don't cancel, I will receive 4 brand-new novels every month and be billed just $4.74 per book in the U.S. or $4.96 per book in Canada. That's a savings of at least 14% off the cover price. It's quite a bargain. Shipping and handling is just 50¢ per book in the U.S. and 75¢ per book in Canada.* I understand that accepting the 2 free books and gifts places me under no obligation to buy anything. I can always return a shipment and cancel at any time. Even if I never buy another book, the two free books and gifts are mine to keep forever.

150/350 HDN F4WC

Name _____ (PLEASE PRINT)

Address _____ Apt. #

City _____ State/Prov. _____ Zip/Postal Code

Signature (if under 18, a parent or guardian must sign)

Mail to the Harlequin® Reader Service:
IN U.S.A.: P.O. Box 1867, Buffalo, NY 14240-1867
IN CANADA: P.O. Box 609, Fort Erie, Ontario L2A 5X3

Want to try two free books from another line?
Call 1-800-873-8635 or visit www.ReaderService.com.

* Terms and prices subject to change without notice. Prices do not include applicable taxes. Sales tax applicable in N.Y. Canadian residents will be charged applicable taxes. Offer not valid in Quebec. This offer is limited to one order per household. Not valid for current subscribers to Harlequin Blaze books. All orders subject to credit approval. Credit or debit balances in a customer's account(s) may be offset by any other outstanding balance owed by or to the customer. Please allow 4 to 6 weeks for delivery. Offer available while quantities last.

Your Privacy—The Harlequin® Reader Service is committed to protecting your privacy. Our Privacy Policy is available online at www.ReaderService.com or upon request from the Harlequin Reader Service.

We make a portion of our mailing list available to reputable third parties that offer products we believe may interest you. If you prefer that we not exchange your name with third parties, or if you wish to clarify or modify your communication preferences, please visit us at www.ReaderService.com/consumerschoice or write to us at Harlequin Reader Service Preference Service, P.O. Box 9062, Buffalo, NY 14269. Include your complete name and address.

SPECIAL EXCERPT FROM

◆ **H HARLEQUIN**

Blaze

Here's a sneak peek at

A SEAL's Secret

by Tawny Weber,
part of the ***Uniformly Hot!*** miniseries.

Halloween

"My, oh, my, talk about temptation. A room filled with
sexy SEALs, an abundance of alcohol and deliciously fat-
tening food."

Olivia Kane cast an appreciative look around Olive Oyl's,
the funky bar that catered to the local naval base and locals
alike. She loved the view of the various temptations, even
though she knew she wouldn't be indulging in any.

Not that she didn't want to.

She'd love nothing more than to dive into an oversize
margarita and chow down on a plate of fully loaded nachos.
But her career hinged on her body being in prime condi-
tion, so she'd long ago learned to resist empty calories.

And the sexy sailors?

Livi barely kept from pouting. She was pretty sure a
wild bout with a yummy military hunk would do amazing
things for her body, too.

It wasn't willpower that kept her from indulging in that
particular temptation, though. It was shyness, pure and
simple.

But it was Halloween—time for make-believe. And tonight, she was going to pretend she was the kind of woman who had the nerve to hit on a sailor, throw caution to the wind and do wildly sexy things without caring about tomorrow.

"My, oh, my," her friend Tessa murmured. "Now there's a treat I wouldn't mind showing a trick or two."

Livi mentally echoed that with a purr.

Oh, my, indeed.

The room was filled with men, all so gorgeous that they blurred into a yummy candy store in Livi's mind. It was a good night when a woman could choose between a gladiator, a kilted highlander and a bare-chested fireman.

But Livi only had eyes for the superhero.

Deep in conversation with another guy, he might be sitting in the corner, but he still seemed in command of the entire room. He had that power vibe.

And he was a superhottie.

His hair was as black as midnight and brought to mind all sorts of fun things to do at that hour. The supershort cut accentuated the shape of his face with its sharp cheekbones and strong jawline. His eyes were light, but she couldn't tell the color from here. Livi wet her suddenly dry lips and forced her gaze lower, wondering if the rest of him lived up to the promise of that gorgeous face.

Who is this sexy SEAL and what secrets is he hiding? Find out in A SEAL'S SECRET by Tawny Weber.
Available February 2015 wherever Harlequin® Blaze books and ebooks are sold!

HBEXPO115R

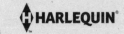